O9-BTJ-901
The Fantastical
Town of
FINKLE
STORE
Graham/Francis

Kids 4 Kids Productions
123 Laurendale Avenue
Waterdown, ON
L0R 2H3
This edition of "The Fantastical Town of Finkle" published 2001
kids@kids4kids.ca

ISBN 0-9689062-0-6

THE FANTASTICAL REVIEWS

"THE BEST CHILDREN'S BOOK OF THE YEAR..."

The Finkle Weekly

"FINALLY, A PIECE OF CHILDREN'S LITERATURE THAT ALL AGES CAN ENJOY."

Freda Finklestein

"I LAUGHED SO HARD MY BELLY ACHED FOR AN HOUR!"

Ima Laffen

"VALUABLE LIFE LESSONS ARE TAUGHT IN THE TOWN OF FINKLE. LET'S HOPE WE CAN ALL LEARN FROM THEM."

Chico Chic-olet

"ADVENTURE, SUSPENSE, MYSTERY AND HUMOR WRAPPED UP IN ONE BOOK. I LOVE IT!"

Freud Ian Shlip - Principal Of Milmac Public School

CONTENTS

To AMANDA, ANTHONY, DOMINIC,
WILL, HALLE AND GABRIELLE

BAKED BEANS, BANANA BREATH, BOATS AND BURNING BOTTOMS

Chapter 1

Eric and the Green Gorilla decided to take a well-deserved rest in the Finkle Mountains to recover from the people that made up the fantastical town of Finkle. You see, Finkle was a town like no other. It was north of someplace, south of nothing and in the middle of nowhere. There are tales of swamp creatures, buried treasure, a hangman's tower, Amazon vacations, bullies and much more.

The people of Finkle are even stranger than the stories they created. The only person who knows all of the stories of this town is Eric, a vertically challenged ex-bully who has the gift of gab. Even Eric had his part in creating an unbelievable adventure involving his new found friend, the Green Gorilla.

"Come on Eric, tell me another story about the fantastical town of Finkle. Sitting here around the campfire, roasting bananas and enjoying the peace and quiet of the outdoors is nothing without a good story. What do you say?"

"I'll make you a deal Banana-breath. You place those boats you call feet down wind of me and I'll tell you as many stories as I can remember. Between your Banana-breath and your Gorilla feet I feel like I'm going to pass out."

"No Problem Eric! Let me finish making my big Banana Boat before you start your stories. I am going to put marshmallows, chocolate sauce, candy sprinkles and whipping cream into my banana boat, wrap it up in foil, cook it in the fire for five minutes, then sail it right down into my stomach. I learned the art of ice cream creations from Kris Kafoogaloo, a boy I met at Milmac Public School."

"Remember what happened last time Gorilla? You devoured ten Banana Boats in less than ten minutes. You muttered something about not feeling too well, then, boom... Banana Boat mush everywhere! You smelled like banana for a good two weeks. Let's not visit that situation again, alright!" exclaimed Eric.

"I won't eat as many this time. I'm smarter now! I even thought of a way of saving time. I put a can of baked beans on the campfire about five minutes ago. I just have to open the can and presto, Beans ala Gorilla."

"You can't put a can of beans on an open fire. They will...

B-o-o-M

explode! Green Gorilla, you did it to me again. Now I'm covered head to toe with beans! You're driving me crazy!"

"Sorry Eric. Maybe you should start the story of the town of Finkle and it's people?" begged the Green Gorilla.

"Good idea! I think I'll begin with the story about your friend, Kris Kafoogaloo and the time he experienced No Rule Day. Maybe you'll learn

something that will actually prevent you from covering me with your next concoction."

"I'm so excited! I can't contain myself. I'll just sit over here near the fire," exclaimed the Gorilla.

"Watch you don't sit too close," said Eric.

"What's that smell," asked the Green Gorilla. "It smells like burnt fur."

"I told you not to sit so close to the fire. Your bottom is burning!" yelled Eric.

The Green Gorilla danced around the campsite for a good five minutes before he was able to put out the flames that were shooting out of his bottom. He had a sore bum for a good week, but still managed to sit and listen to the stories of the fantastical town of Finkle.

No RULE DAY

Chapter 2

It was Monday morning, the first day of school after the Christmas break. Kris Kafoogaloo, a blond-haired, blue-eyed, eight-year-old boy was upstairs in his room, mustering up all his energies to get his slim framed body out of bed. Kris was lying comfortably on his mattress thinking to himself.

"What a bummer! Not only is it another Monday morning, but it is also the first day of school after a holiday!"

You see, Kris had an attitude about school. He just did not want to go. He would come up with many creative excuses as to why it was better to stay at home than go to school. Kris's best excuse was when he told his teacher and his classmates that his pet Tarantula, Hershey, crawled out of its cage and into his dad's underwear drawer. Kris's father went into his drawer to get a pair of underwear. He found Hershey sitting sweetly on his "Fruit of the Looms." His father had a fit! He would have been even angrier if he had put his underwear on with Hershey nestled inside. Hershey wouldn't have been too happy either! As a result, Kris had to spend his entire day washing his dad's clothes. Hershey had gotten excited and peed all over them.

Kris was feeling really bummed out that he had to go back to school. He trudged down the stairs, and almost jumped out of his skin when he heard an ear shattering, "Meowwwwwwww". Kris had almost stepped on Fluffy, the family cat.

"Oh for goodness sake, Fluffy," squealed Kris, "Get off the stairs! I almost stepped on you, you crazy cat!"

Fluffy gave a quick hiss and bounded down the stairs.

Kris popped his head into the kitchen to see whether his mother had made breakfast for him yet.

"Hey mom, what's for breakfast?" he asked with a yawn.

His mother seemed very excited this morning. She was absolutely gushing when she said,

"Didn't you hear the news this morning? Oh, for goodness sake everyone knows... it's "No Rule Day" today! You can have anything you want for breakfast because there are no rules!"

"Anything I want!" Kris shouted, "Anything?"

His mother nodded in agreement and no sooner had her head stopped nodding than Kris was into the refrigerator and freezer. He grabbed the biggest bucket of green slimy Goober ice cream (which was his absolute favorite!) and piled it high into a huge bowl. He took a can of whipped cream from the refrigerator and squirted until the can was empty! Plewwwtrp! What a great sight, a mountain of cream! Then, he sprinkled on Gummy Bears, Hershey Kisses and Smarties until the whipped cream was totally covered! However, he was not finished yet. Where was the chocolate sauce? He knew his mother had bought chocolate sauce. There it was, right at the back of the refrigerator.

"Got it!"

Now his breakfast was complete! He went for a spoon, but realized they were all in the dishwasher.

"Oh, great!" thought Kris. "How am I going to eat my breakfast?"

Kris thought about it being "No Rule Day" and decided that he could do anything he wanted. He used his hands to devour his colossal creation. He attacked the huge sundae until there was nothing left in the bottom of the bowl but leftover slime. When Kris had finished, he was a mess! He had green, slimy ice cream and chocolate sauce all over his face and a stream of whipped cream oozing from the end of his nose. Moreover, hanging on for dear life, from the end of his right nostril, was a half-eaten Gummy Bear!

Since it was "No Rule Day" Kris decided that he did not need to wash up after breakfast or brush his teeth. So, he didn't! His mother turned around to tell him that he had better hurry if he wanted to catch the school bus and let out a shriek when she saw his disgusting green, slimy face!

"I thought you were some sort of alien! For goodness sakes, run upstairs and get changed right this minute!" his mother yelled.

Kris was not too thrilled with the idea of going to school, but knowing that it was "No

Rule Day" he thought that maybe school would be a bit of an adventure! He started up the stairs, stepping over Fluffy this time (who hadn't learned his lesson from earlier), and skipped into his bedroom. He looked out his window to check on the weather, only to be confronted with a major snowstorm! It looked wickedly cold outside.

"Hmmm," he thought to himself, "I wonder what I should wear to school today?"

Kris scratched his head and looked in his closet. Nothing caught his eye until he opened his dresser drawer and came up with a brilliant idea! Kris started rummaging through his clothes until he found what he was looking for.

"That's what I will wear... my Barney bathing suit. It's F-U-N-K-Y!"

So he put on his Barney bathing suit, wrapped a Pongaroo beach towel around his neck, and put on his cool neon sunglasses!

"I'm cool... and I'm ready to go!" he said to himself.

Kris started down the stairs, humming one of his favorite tunes, and of course, forgetting that Fluffy was still on the stairs.

S-Q-U-I-S-H !

"Oh, no - Fluffy! Somebody call 911!"

Kris started CPR and artificial respiration, but it was no use.

"I guess we'll have to start calling you Squishy from now on. Just get off the bottom of my shoe, will you, you crazy cat!"

Kris skidded into the kitchen where his mother was waiting at the door to see him off to school. Her chin dropped to the floor as she looked at her son in disbelief.

"You're going to go out in a snowstorm dressed like THAT? In a bathing suit?"

Kris grinned from ear to ear. "Yeah, isn't it cool!"

His mother just shook her head, laughed and said, "You're going to be cool alright. Well, have a nice day at school and a nice walk as well, because you just missed your bus!"

Kris could not believe the school bus had gone, but thought it would be fun anyway to walk to school in the snow in his awesomely cool Barney bathing suit! He was sure that no one else would be brave enough to wear their Barney bathing suit in a snowstorm! He was going to be the bravest!

Kris opened the door and was blasted with snow and wind from the raging snowstorm. The blast of wind sent an instant message that maybe it was not such a good idea to walk through the snow with bare legs.

"What the heck" thought Kris, "I'll show everyone who's cool!"

He started walking to school, fighting the wind all the way. His legs began stiffening as they turned different shades of blue. There were icicles hanging from his nose and his lips were frozen shut! Kris was so cool he was almost frozen!

When Kris walked through the doors of Milmac Public School, he nearly traumatized a small group of kindergarten children. They thought some sort of Abominable Snow Walrus was invading their school. Kris walked around the freaked-out five-year-olds and stood for a good hour in the front hallway until he had thawed out!

All of a sudden, Kris heard a noise coming from the hall where his classroom was. He slowly turned the corner and looked down the hall, but didn't see anyone. That wasn't too strange as he did miss his bus and was more than an hour late for class. Everyone must be in class, he thought, but where was all that strange noise coming from? He walked down the hall and into his classroom, blue legs and all, only to find his teacher, Mrs. Finklestein, tied up to her chair in the corner. His classmates were screaming as they shot paper airplanes, elastics, and spitballs at each other. They were running up and down the aisles, hopping from desktop to desktop!

A huge grin appeared on Kris's face. This was going to be an amazing day!

After playing with some of his friends, he decided it would be totally cool to play on the computer. After all, there were no rules today so he could play on the computer all day long if he wanted to! A girl had been sitting at the computer all morning so Kris went up to her (her name was Penelope Puker... aaagghh, gross!)

"Au, Penelope, I think you've been on the computer long enough. You have to share, you know, like co-operate and take turns, that kind of stuff!"

Kris got a real shock when Penelope turned to him and said, "No, I don't think so. It's "No Rule Day" today. I can do anything I want, and I want to play on the computer! I don't have to share, cooperate, or do anything I'm asked to do on "No Rule Day", so see ya, wouldn't want to be ya!"

Kris didn't know what to think. What a drag! He knew Penelope was right, after all; it was "No Rule Day!"

"Oh well, no big deal," he thought, "I'll just go do something else."

Kris went to the corner where the Lego was and started to build a huge Lego tower. He built it so big that it towered over his head.

From down the hall... he heard something coming! It was rumbling closer and closer to the classroom. It was big, and it was loud. All the kids in the class were running to the corners of the classroom, hiding under desks, and behind curtains. Kris couldn't figure out what was going on. The door of the classroom suddenly opened with a deafening CRASH! There in the doorway was Billy Booger, the biggest and nastiest schoolyard bully you have ever seen!

Billy immediately spied the huge tower that Kris had built and made his way across the classroom.

"Hey, that's a pretty cool tower, kid. Too bad I'm going to have to BREAK IT!"

Down it came, every single piece of Kris's incredible structure.

Kris was a little more than upset now, and yelled, "What did you do that for? I've spent the entire morning working on this tower!"

Billy puffed out his chest and said, "It's No Rule Day today and I can do anything I want and no one can stop me! I can break things, call people names, bully and hurt people. What are you going to do about it? Get it! It's No Rule Day... don't you just love it?"

Kris thought to himself that this "No Rule Day" was turning out to be a real drag.

R-r-r-ing... It was the lunch bell.

"Finally," sighed Kris; "at least I'll get a good lunch!"

He walked into the lunchroom, drooling over the thought of the awesome lunch he was about to digest, as his mother always made really amazing lunches for him, like pizza, submarine sandwiches and sometimes even delicious hamburgers! Kris couldn't wait to see what she'd made for him today! He opened his lunch pail to see a delicious... hairy raisin? There was nothing in his lunch pail! Nothing except... a... tiny... little... hairy... RAISIN?

"What the heck am I going to do with a tiny hairy raisin!" he yelled. He turned to the boy beside him and said, "I'll trade you my hairy raisin for a piece of your pizza."

"Get lost! Not a chance," said Lenny, the red haired, freckle-faced boy who never shared anything.

Kris decided that he had to make the best of it so he popped the raisin into his mouth and started sucking on it. As it softened, he thought that it tasted somewhat weird for a raisin. It had an awfully sour taste.

"Wait a minute! What's this in my mouth?"

Kris put his fingers to his mouth and pulled out... a wing! No, wait... there was two wings! Wings? Two wings on a hairy raisin? "Oh, gross! I'm going to puke! I think I just ate a fly!"

He screamed as he ran to the lunchroom sink. Everyone was ducking for cover in case Kris began to throw up.

"Forget the sink," he thought, "I need to get to the nurse's office!"

So, there he was lying in the nurse's office, moaning and groaning away... "Ohhhhh. Ughhh. Agggghh."

The bell rang, ending yet another lunch hour. The kindergarten kids were all lined up and were beginning to walk past the nurse's room. They heard strange sounds and started whispering to each other that there was a monster in the nurse's room!

Their teacher overheard them and said, "Don't be silly, there are no such things as monsters."

One of the brave little kindergarten boys, whose name was Calvin, decided to look around the corner of the nurse's room. He looked at the bed where the noise was coming from only to see a green, slimy ice cream-faced boy with a Gummy Bear hanging from his nose and Smarties smashed into chocolate sauce all around his mouth! Kris let out a gut wrenching groan that catapulted Calvin straight toward the roof. When Calvin landed, he was spinning in his tracks.

"Aaagghhh!!" screamed Calvin, "there IS a monster in there!"

Calvin tore out of the nurse's room almost losing his pants on the corner of the door. He started running in circles as the rest of the kindergarten class scattered all over the floor, bumping into teachers, tables and knocking over

anything in their way! Calvin ran right over Susie who was standing in his way.

"I think I got a Nike in the nose!" moaned Susie.

Kris got up from the nurse's bed and walked toward the door.

"What the devil is everyone's problem? Well, I don't care! I feel gross and I'm going home."

Kris walked all the way back home in the freezing cold with his green, slimy, chocolate and dried-whipped-creamed face. Icicles were forming on his nose and his legs were turning blue all over again. He walked through the back door of his house to find his mother sitting in the kitchen reading the paper.

"So, how was your "No Rule Day," today?" his mother asked.

Kris was almost in tears as he said, "Don't ask me about my No Rule Day. I hated it! First, I had to walk to school with this really gross breakfast in my stomach and I felt so sick. Not only that, but it was freezing outside. My legs were almost frozen together! I was so cold that I began walking as if I was some sort of creature from one of those old monster movies. When I finally got to school everyone was screaming and yelling. The noise gave me a pounding headache. There were no teachers around anywhere, or if there were, they were all tied up. When I tried to get on the computer, this girl, Penelope, wouldn't cooperate or share so I didn't get to use it. Then, I built a cool tower and Billy, the biggest bully the school has ever seen broke it. I couldn't get any help from my teacher because she was tied up in the corner! By then it was time to eat so I went to lunch and all I could find in my lunch pail was a raisin which turned out to be a FLY! Thanks very much, mom! Then I had to go to the nurse's room because I was feeling like I was about to lose my lunch, which I never really had! I was such a mess and was making so many groaning noises I ended up scaring a bunch of kindergarten kids. Well, actually, that was kind of fun! To top it all off, I had to walk back home, in the freezing cold, in only my Barney bathing suit. With everything that happened to me today, I think that "No Rule Day" is a real drag, and I hated it!"

Kris ran out of the kitchen and up the stairs past Squishy, to his bedroom. He threw his towel on the floor, and climbed into his warm bed and fell asleep.

It didn't seem like he had been asleep very long when he woke up with a start! Kris looked around his room and realized that it was morning. Wait a minute! All the "No Rule Day" stuff was just a dream? He jumped out of bed and put on his warmest clothes. He stepped over Fluffy on the stairs, and got to the kitchen to find an amazing breakfast waiting for him! This is the way it should be! He grabbed his coat, hopped on the bus and got to school in record time. At school he got to play on the computer and worked with another kid to build this amazing Lego wall! Billy Booger tried to tease Kris, but the teacher stopped his bullying attack, sending Billy to the office! Kris had pizza, fruit, pop and a special snack for lunch. Life was good!

As Kris was munching away on his brownie, he realized that rules are made to protect you. Rules help make sure you get your share, that no one takes advantage of you and consequently, you can feel good about yourself and others. So, actually, ***Rules Are Cool!*** Kris also realized that school was a great place to be as you could meet new friends, learn new and exciting things and help others learn that rules are cool and important for everyone!

To TELL oR NoT To TELL

Chapter 3

"That was a great story Eric, but how about the story about the time we met? I scared you so bad that you peed your pants and begged me not to pummel you. You said you would change your ways from being a bully to being a leader."

"Did you have to bring that up? You know that I learned my lesson about hurting people with my words and actions. Brutus and Billy, the town bullies would love to pay me back for all of my taunts with their super-sonic wedgie!"

"When you tell me the story pretend it's about someone else. No one will know it's your story. Instead of using your real last name, use an alias. If Brutus and Billy hear you telling the story, they won't realize it's you that you're talking about. You can be Eric Crunchurlunch."

"That's a great idea, Green Gorilla! I rather like telling the story. Eric Crunchurlunch it is! I'll even tell you about a few other characters I know from Finkle. So, put those stinky, banana boat feet of yours up and listen. You won't believe what I am about to tell you."

ERIC AND THE GREEN GORILLA

Chapter 4

Eric Crunchurlunch was the meanest bully at Milmac Public School. His breath was bad and so was he. He was even meaner than Billy Booger! Eric was a red-haired, freckle-faced warrior, with a reputation that followed him everywhere he went. He wore the baggiest poopy pants you have ever seen, with rips down the backside, which revealed his commando-styled boxers. His victims were usually younger, smaller, and of course, weaker. He especially enjoyed taunting kids who did not have it in them to fight back or stand up for themselves. Eric thought that the reactions he received from his victims made him cool. He also thought that being tough earned him respect. Boy, was he wrong!

It was the beginning of another school week. Eric would arrive early every morning, as this was prime bullying time. He would make his way from one side of the playground to the other, destroying children with the power of his words. Eric could never understand how people could be so naïve to believe that: "Sticks and stones can break your bones, but names can never hurt you." After all, Eric knew that words could hurt forever.

As Eric walked over his usual number of casualties, he caught sight of Mrs. Finklestein. Mrs. Finklestein was the only teacher Eric feared. She knew his type and knew exactly how to disempower him.

"Knowledge is the key to conquering your fear of bullies," she would drone.

That's all Eric needed! If Eric's victims ever found out that all bullies want is reactions, attention and the ability to control others, he would lose his reputation as the meanest bully in the school. Eric needed to prove that he was the meanest bully that Finkle Public School had ever seen. But, how?

Eric decided to skip school. He tried to talk his buddies into skipping school, but they were also afraid of Mrs. Finklestein. The last time Eric and his friends were caught skipping school, Mrs. Finklestein went ballistic. It was not a pretty sight. She made King Kong look like a sissy.

Most of Eric's so-called friends were not actually friends at all, but kids who were afraid of being bullied. After all, the safest place to be if you don't want to be bullied is with the bully, right?

Eric had heard that there were ferocious animals from the jungles of Africa at the local zoo this week. They drew fear into the heart of the bravest man. Eric had a plan. He was going to taunt and tease these animals into a frenzy. There would be such a ruckus that everyone at Milmac Public would hear about it. There would be no way that Eric would lose his reputation as the meanest kid at school. If he could bully these wild animals even "knowledge" would be no match for his bullying antics.

Although Eric acted big on the outside, with his leather jacket, earring, and dark sunglasses, in fact he felt small and insecure. Like many bullies, Eric was the victim of bullying himself. He was bullied and constantly put down by his older brother. Eric's father wasn't much better. He bullied everyone, including Eric. It was easy to see where Eric had learned his bullying techniques. Eric also had a problem with reading. He was very self-conscious about it and thought that if he got the reputation for being the worst kid in school no one would dare tease him about his inability to read.

Eric told his friends they were all a bunch of chickens and said he was going to go to the zoo by himself. He wanted to see the man-eating wolves, white tigers, and huge snakes that could actually swallow you whole and spit out your bones! That was cool!

Eric hopped on the local bus and rode to the zoo. As he sneaked through the main gates of the zoo, he noticed a large group of people coming out of a big tent. They all looked extremely pale. They were moving quickly as if they had seen something that they would rather be far away from. This made Eric curious. He had to see what had terrified these people.

Eric quickly maneuvered his short, over-Twinkied body through the crowd, past the ticket taker and into the tent. Eric stood in the middle of the tent, staring at a cage that held the biggest gorilla he had ever seen. It was 8 feet tall, 4 feet wide and green! It had the goofiest expression on its face. It kept asking Eric if he had any bananas. Eric couldn't believe that the two hundred pounds of bananas it had just eaten wasn't enough. Eric got an evil grin on his face and thought to himself how cool it would be to tease the Green Gorilla. He would get the gorilla to react, which would cement his reputation as the meanest bully into eternity.

Without fear, Eric walked right up to the cage where the Green Gorilla was looking out and yelled, "Hey, Gorilla... Do you take baths with Pepi Le Pew because... YOU STINK!!"

The gorilla looked a little confused, looked around and nonchalantly smelled under his armpits. With an eu-wee and a wild shriek the Green Gorilla grunted something about rotting bananas, rolled his eyes, and motioned to Eric that he thought he might pass out! NEVERTHELESS, the gorilla didn't react to the teasing. This had never happened before!

"All the kids always get angry, upset or afraid when I tease them," thought Eric. "What's going on?"

Without thinking, Eric grabbed the keys to the gorilla's cage from the sleeping attendant and opened it up. Eric walked right up to the gorilla and delivered his second tease attack.

"Hey, Bubblebutt! Your rear is the biggest thing I've ever seen! It's as big as a bus!"

Now Eric thought for sure that he would get a reaction from the gorilla. Instead, the gorilla looked at his rear-end, looked a little confused, but totally unconcerned. Eric was really beginning to worry.

"What if I'm losing my touch," he thought to himself. "What happens if people find that I've lost my touch and that I can't read and I get bullied?"

Eric looked over each shoulder to make sure nobody had noticed his failed teasing attacks. He decided that no one had seen him, so he quietly backed his way out of the gorilla cage. As Eric was backing out of the cage, he accidentally tripped over a rubber hose, and stumbled, not towards the cage door, but toward the Green Gorilla. In doing so, he ended up touching the Green Gorilla on the head. The gorilla's facial expression immediately changed.

The Gorilla released a toe-curling scream. "I want bananas! You got bananas!"

Eric had never come as close to wetting his pants as he did during that experience!

Eric turned and started to run as fast as his wobbly legs would carry him. The gorilla was a little startled by Eric's fast departure, but pushed his way past the pile of banana peels in pursuit of his new found friend, Eric. Eric was running as fast as he could, up and down the paved aisles of the zoo. Past the polar bear exhibit, through the bird pavilion, around the "Swim With The Piranha Show", but always, the gorilla was right behind him. Eric could not lose the gorilla no matter how hard he tried. Finally, he made a break for the front gate, up through the lion's den, across the alligator pit, racing towards the car park. Eric tried the first car, then the second, and finally, at the third, the door opened and Eric jumped inside. He slammed the locks down. At least he was safe for the time being,

but he had to get out of there! This was definitely Eric's lucky day... dangling from the ignition were the keys! Eric turned the keys, and put the pedal to the metal and burned rubber. Eric was not exactly the most experienced driver so he rolled down the window to make sure he didn't run over anything. Before he mastered his driving technique he had bowled over a group of old ladies and skimmed through the penguin pond. Eric noticed a penguin sitting quite comfortably beside him.

"I can't have a penguin in the car!" screamed Eric. He picked up the penguin and threw it out the window.

"Oops! I thought penguins could fly!" he thought to himself. "Sorry about that," he yelled to the penguin. "I am having a bad day!"

Eric noticed that the car was slowing. At first he thought he was running out of gas, but then he heard a scraping sound behind him. What was that? He looked in the rear view mirror to find the Green Gorilla hanging on for dear life to the bumper of the car!

"Aaaggghh!!" screamed Eric.

Eric slammed on the brakes, catapulting the Green Gorilla over the front of the car, bumping off the hood, and coming down on some poor old granny.

As the Green Gorilla pulled himself up Eric overheard him say, "Granny is kinda squishy. So sorry, must go now."

Eric had had enough of driving. He jumped out of the car and started running for his life. Of course, hot on his trail was the Green Gorilla. Eric made it to the train station and hopped on the only train leaving the station at that time. The doors of the train closed just as the Green Gorilla hit them. Splat! The Green Gorilla's face was sandwiched against the window as the train started down the track. Eric was heading for Unionville, but it was better than having to deal with the Green Gorilla!

Eric found a seat and felt safe for the first time since opening the gorilla's cage. The feeling of safety, however, lasted for only a moment because Eric was sure someone was watching him. It was an awful feeling! Turning his head to the right, his eyes met those of a haggard old, squished granny lady sitting beside him. She looked as if she was having a bad hair day. Eric looked to his left to see beautiful farm fields filled with brown mounds of dirt and hay. Eric noticed that there were tiny green things attached to the bottom of the train window. All of a sudden, the Green Gorilla's faced popped up.

"Aaaaggghhhh!" Eric screamed.

The gorilla's face was plastered against the window. The Green Gorilla started making funny faces against the windowpane.

"I want ba-na-nas," yelled the gorilla.

The sight of the Green Gorilla looking through the glass almost made Eric lose his lunch. He had to escape. He bolted out of his seat and ran for the door. Eric opened the emergency door and thought that if he closed his eyes and counted to ten he could jump and land in one of the soft piles of hay. Eric closed his eyes and mustered up all his courage. He threw his body off the train, directing it toward the softest area he could see.

Splat! Eric landed in the softest, warmest pile of cow manure in the field!

"Gross! This STINKS!" Eric gasped.

Not to be defeated quite yet, the Green Gorilla jumped off the train landing in the same pile of manure. There was cow poopy flying everywhere. The gorilla got up and started chasing Eric again. Eric could not believe that the Green Gorilla was still following him. He was getting awfully tired of having this big green galoot of a gorilla bullying him! It was time to take emergency measures! Eric ran through a farmer's field, heading straight for a humming sound coming from the next field over. Eric knew that sound. He had been taking some flying lessons with his Uncle Fester, so he was quite familiar with the sounds of an airfield! Eric climbed the fence and took a quick look behind him. There, rumbling through the field, not more than three football fields away was the Green Gorilla! Would this gorilla never give up?

As Eric reached the first plane hangar he saw what he was looking for... a small single engine, two-seater plane. This was similar to the one his uncle had been showing him how to fly. Eric thought he had had enough lessons to know how to fly it, and by the looks of things, this was going to be the only way to lose that gorilla once and for all! Hopping up on the wing, Eric crawled to the door and climbed into the pilot's seat. Starting the plane, Eric taxied out onto the little runway and asked for permission to take off. As permission was granted, Eric noticed that the Green Gorilla was nowhere to be seen.

"Maybe he didn't see where I went", thought Eric. "Maybe now I'll be able to go home and be left in peace!"

Eric was beginning to regret ever having teased and bullied the gorilla, but soon, he would be home safely and he would have won!

As Eric taxied down the runway and revved his engine, he noticed that the plane was a little sluggish as it tried to lift off.

"That's strange," thought Eric, "it's almost like there's an additional weight on board."

Eric looked around the cockpit as he was ascending into the air, but noticed nothing unusual. All the instruments were telling him that he was okay and that all his systems were 'go', so who knows, maybe it was just his imagination. Maybe a quick visual check of his wings would be a good idea. Eric turned to check his left wing and found no problems there, but as he turned to his right wing he noticed a piece of green fur caught in one of the flaps!

"Oh, no!" exclaimed Eric; "this can't be true!"

But it was, for there on the wing, as Eric flew the plane, the Green Gorilla was hanging on to one of the struts and dancing on the wing! It was doing the Gorilla Cha-Cha.

"He's making fun of me!" cried Eric.

Well, enough was enough. It was time to get rid of this big green fur ball. Eric flew upside down and sideways, and rolled over several times but still the gorilla hung on. Eric flew straight up and then straight down, but the gorilla was still there.

"I want bananas!" was all that was heard as the Green Gorilla hung on to the wing of the plane for dear life.

Eric wasn't paying close attention to exactly where he was until it was too late... there in front of him was Milmac Public School and all the kids were just getting out of class.

"Oh, no, who's that on the front lawn with the principal?" murmured Eric. "Could it be my home room teacher, Mrs. Finklestein? It is Mrs. Finklestein!"

With a mischievous grin Eric dropped altitude and buzzed past his school, the principal and Mrs. Finklestein! Everyone but Mrs. Finklestein ducked as Eric flew overhead. Mrs. Finklestein just stood there in horror as her dress flew up over her head! What a sight... oh, my!

"Enough fun," thought Eric, "I'm getting tired of having to fight off this gorilla! I'm going to get out of here and let the gorilla try to fly the plane!"

Eric put the plane on autopilot and put on his parachute. Opening the pilot's door, Eric jumped out and waved 'good-bye' to the Green Gorilla. Finally, he had outsmarted the old fur ball!

"I guess I'm not losing my touch after all," exclaimed Eric as he floated towards the ground. However, one thing that Eric couldn't have known was that Green Gorillas could fly!

Seeing Eric jump from the plane, the Green Gorilla decided that it was time to leave the plane as well, although he had been having quite a good time dancing on the wing! As Eric touched down on the ground, the parachute covered his head and he didn't see the gorilla coming down after him. As Eric emerged from the silk of the parachute, he heard a 'thud' not more than 50 feet away.

"What on earth was that?" questioned Eric.

Looking out from the mounds of silk Eric saw the Green Gorilla get up and start brushing himself off!

"How could it be... how could he have followed me down here?" wondered Eric.

Just then, Eric heard voices discussing the amazing descent of the Green Gorilla... and then he knew... Green Gorillas could fly! Eric could not stand it any longer. Turning to where the gorilla had landed, he yelled, "Okay, Banana Breath, I give up!"

The Green Gorilla approached Eric and towered over him, just staring at Eric with its huge orange eyes! The Green Gorilla was so big that he almost blocked out the sun! Eric cowered in the grass with his hands tightly covering his head. He realized that his teasing had gone too far this time. With a hand quick as lightning, and as big as a shovel, the Green Gorilla reached out, and gently touched Eric on the shoulder and yelled, ***"Gotcha! You're it!"***

"Are you trying to tell me that all this time you were playing tag with me?" Eric exclaimed.

The Green Gorilla smiled and nodded his head, reaching out his hand to help Eric up. Eric couldn't believe that a Green Gorilla had outsmarted him!

From that day on Eric never teased or bullied anyone again. He now realized what it felt like to be teased and bullied. Eric had never fully realized the effect teasing and bullying had on a person, although he was bullied at home. Eric had always thought that it was the only way to gain power and control. The Green Gorilla, who was now known as the "Gotcha" Gorilla, wanted to give Eric a bit of his own medicine. He wanted Eric to realize how he was making others feel and that there were other ways to gain power and control in one's life.

As time went on, Eric lost his reputation as the school bully. Kids started seeing the real Eric, and the real Eric was pretty cool. With the help of Eric's new friend, the Gotcha Gorilla, he improved his ability to read and began to teach the importance of not bullying others. He started reading books about the fantastical town of Finkle. He found stories filled with mystery, suspense and intrigue. His favorite story was that of Bobby Bubblebutt.

BoBBY BUBBLEBUTT

Chapter 5

The school bell rang, as it usually did, signaling the kids of Milmac Public School that classes were about to begin. Everyone was talking about this new kid from Arkansas, who was supposedly arriving today. Mrs. Finklestein had been preparing the class all week. They weren't exactly sure what all the fuss was about, but they were sure going to find out. As the class herded into the classroom, they all noticed this strange-looking character sitting at the back of the class. He was wearing bright green, over-sized poopy pants, a shirt that looked like he might have wrestled his granny for it, and strange, round-toed, honky-tonk, funky-looking shoes which looked like they belonged in the circus. It took Mrs. Finklestein a few seconds before she invited the new kid from Arkansas up to the front of the class.

"Class," Mrs. Finklestein announced, "this is your new classmate, Bobby Bubblebutt."

Bobby gave a wave, wiped his nose with his sleeve, and squeaked out "Hi guys." The class instantly burst into fits of laughter. Leaky Larry was bursting at the seams and rolled out of the class. Wheezy Willy almost collapsed from an asthma attack, and Big Haired Suzie almost choked on a monster-sized hairball. There were never so many random acts of "Bubble-Butting" heard at Milmac Public School as there were that day. Even Mrs. Finklestein was having difficulty restraining herself. Bobby was very embarrassed and, of course, discouraged, as he was getting tired of always being the "Butt" of everyone's jokes. All he wanted was to be accepted for who he was. He could change his name, but he felt that it was part of who he was and didn't want to change that.

The school bullies, Brutus and Billy Wheacher, decided that Bobby would make an excellent target. Their plan was to dare Bobby to do something stupid. They would promise him friendship in exchange for the dare. This was a promise they had no intention of keeping.

"Hey, Bobby, how would you like to hang out with us? We are the coolest guys in school. You can be one of us. What do you say?" asked Brutus.

"I've never been part of a cool group before," whined Bobby, "I would do almost anything to be cool!"

"It's funny you should say that" squeaked Billy, 'cause we want you to prove to us that you are worthy of being cool."

Brutus and Billy promised Bobby that he could be part of their gang if he did a "Dare." Now everyone at Milmac Public School knew that the word "dare" started with the letter "D" and so did the word "dumb," but unfortunately Bobby didn't realize that this dare was just a way for guys like Brutus and Billy to get him to do the "dumb" thing. He so desperately wanted to be accepted that he was willing to do anything.

"Alright," stammered Bobby, "What is the dare?"

Bobby was dared to go down the well at Squeemy MacDurmit 's farm. The farm had been deserted for years and no one dared to go anywhere near MacDurmit's farm as MacDurmit was known as an evil man who had suddenly disappeared. No one knew for sure where he went. Some people said that he still lurked within the ruins of his farm, waiting for unsuspecting intruders. MacDurmit's well was very deep, and to date, everyone had chickened out at the last minute. No one had gone into the well... but Bobby didn't know that.

The bullies told Bobby that everyone in school, even the girls, had gone down the well! They said that everyone was brave enough to do the dare. But the truth was, no one had ever gone down the well. Brutus and Billy just wanted to see if they could get Bobby to do the dare. They had no intentions of being his friend; they just wanted him to look foolish in front of the other kids.

So Bobby went with Brutus and Billy to MacDurmit's farm. It was a cold and dark evening, with the wind howling through the cracks and crevices of the hollowed out buildings they passed. They had to travel along a narrow dirt path that led toward the farmhouse. No one had travelled this path for years. As they drew closer, feelings of fear filled their souls.

There was no turning back now. As they turned the last corner of the twisted lane they noticed the tombstones that edged the path which led to the house. The sight of the house was enough to send the bravest boy running home, but there was a job to do and that was to see if this new kid, Bobby was actually going to climb down MacDurmit's well!

Bobby, Brutus and Billy pushed past an old wooden gate and walked up a foot path that was over-grown with weeds. The path led around the back of the house where the old well stood. It looked as if it was about to fall apart. It was made of ancient field stone fastened together with red creek mud. There was an old wooden bucket hanging by a frayed rope. The boys looked down the well, but were unable to see very much except a deep, dark abyss. The only things they could see were roots growing out from the side of the well and the only sounds they could hear were of insects crawling up the sides. None of them knew how deep the well actually was, but Bobby was soon to find out. He crawled over the edge of the wall, knocking a few rocks into the darkness. There was no sound of the rocks hitting the bottom.

Bobby grabbed on to the tattered rope and began lowering himself down into the darkness.

The wind seemed to be howling louder as Bobby descended into the depths of the well. All that was heard from the well was the sound of Bobby screaming at the discovery of the many spiders and bats which lived within the well.

"I think an earwig has just crawled into my pants" screamed Bobby. "Get me out of here!"

Within minutes of Bobby's descent there was an eerie silence. Brutus and Billy cautiously peered into the well only to hear a blood-curdling scream as Bobby fell deep into the darkness. It was as if MacDurmit's well had swallowed Bobby! Brutus and Billy looked at each other in horror. They did not know what to do. They turned around and ran as fast as they could for home. They figured that Bobby was done for, and they sure didn't want to take the blame!

Neither Brutus nor Billy were able to sleep very well that night. They both had recurring dreams of being sucked into the blackness of MacDurmit's well and encountering the ghost of MacDurmit himself. What were they going to do?

The next day at school during gym class, Brutus and Billy were playing a game of basketball. They were trying to figure out what they should do about Bobby when all of a sudden they heard a very weird noise coming from under the gym stage. It sounded like a voice whispering their names.

"Brutus... Billy... Brutus... Billy."

Brutus and Billy had to investigate. They walked up to the stage and opened the doors beneath it. The voice seemed to be drawing the boys toward the back of the stage. Brutus and Billy crouched down and edged their way through the mouth of the stage door that seemed to swallow them in its darkness. As they drew closer to the back of the stage, they remembered the legend of the dungeon. It was something most kids didn't think about as the thought of it would run chills down your spine. It was said the school had been built on the site of a dungeon which was part of old Fort Guthery. The dungeons had served as a torture chamber and had been destroyed during the Civil War. Of course no one really believed the story, and because they were real "tough guys" nothing was going to stop them from investigating!

There, to their amazement, in the back wall was an opening. They couldn't believe what they saw! They crawled through and found that they could stand up. In front of them was a long, winding passage with a dirt floor and tall flaming torches lining the walls. There were barred cells that held the remains of the anguished souls of long ago. The legend of the dungeon really was true! They were in the secret dungeon! There was an eerie feeling around them. Speechless, they were wondering who had lit the torches which sent looming shadows through the murky halls, revealing the torment that was expressed on the skulls of the unlucky prisoners.

As they neared the end of the long, winding passageway they heard a noise. At first they thought it was one of the many rats which were running about their feet, but it seemed to be the same whispering sound that drew them both into the passage in the first place. They decided to follow the noise which led them farther into the darkness, moving cautiously as they turned every corner. They believed there was safety in numbers, advice they didn't want their victims to understand. The passage came to an abrupt end, and out of the shadows appeared a dark figure. The shadow it made on the wall was enormous. The panic stricken boys leaped out of their pants and were left standing in their heart-decorated underwear. The shadowy form slowly stepped into the light. They couldn't believe their eyes, for it was BOBBY BUBBLEBUTT! He was covered in cuts, scrapes and bruises with droplets of blood staining his torn clothing.

Slowly, Bobby approached the petrified pair, whispering two words which Brutus and Billy would not soon forget... "You're mine... !" The words were repeated again and again, and their ears were tortured by the fearsome voice that was accentuated by the dungeon and the hollow echoes within it. The tough boys, cowards after all, tried desperately to run, tripped over themselves several times, then took off along a side passageway only to find that it ended in a cell! The bullies were trapped! Bobby, who had been following them, slammed the cell door shut. Brutus and Billy were now locked in the same cell that had been used to torture the minds and souls of the Civil War prisoners. Bobby looked into the cell and told them it was his turn to "dare" them.

Bobby told the bullies that he never really fell for the dare. He had investigated the dungeon on several occasions during the summer holidays and knew exactly where to go and how to get out. He told his prisoners that he wasn't that dumb to fall for dares, because he knew they are just ways for others to get control over you, and he wasn't about to give that control to anyone. The dare now was to see if Brutus and Billy could survive alone, in the darkness for as long as he did. Both promised that they would never dare anyone again, but it was too late. Bobby was already gone.

The next day, Bobby showed up at school as if nothing had happened; however, the bullies weren't anywhere to be seen. Mrs. Finklestein phoned their homes, but there was no answer. It wasn't unlike Brutus and Billy to skip school, so no one paid too much attention. Fortunately, Bobby didn't want to be like Brutus and Billy. He knew that daring was wrong. So, he decided to tell Mrs. Finklestein where the two boys were. They were let out of the cell and ended up staying home for a week to recover. A week later the bullies showed up for school, but they were totally different. They had glazed looks upon their faces as if they had lived through something that they would never forget. No one knew what had happened to them, but everyone knew that they were different. Both Brutus and Billy had learned a valuable lesson... that daring is dumb and dangerous! Not only could they have hurt Bobby, but they could have hurt themselves as well.

MacDurmit farm is still there, and so are the passageways. If you wish to visit them you can. That's if you *DARE!*

HIDE AND GO FLUSH

Chapter 6

Dirk Dooley was the coolest guy at Milmac Public School, or so he thought. He was as big as an oak and as wide as a barn. His hands were the size of shovels and his shoes were often mistaken for skis. He was BIG! Dirk scared kids into giving him what he wanted. After all, who would argue with this over-sized, over-stuffed bully?

Dirk was known for his ability to taunt and tease other children. He created what he called *Dooley Deeds,* which were taken out on kids who either fought back or freaked out. You would instantly become one of Dirk's main targets if you yelled, screamed, cried or ran to a teacher. Dirk loved controlling others. He loved reactions!

The day Dirk created the Dooley Dare was the day that changed the lives of many children at Finkle. Dirk promised that if you did a "Dooley Dare" you would be guaranteed a spot in the cool group. If you refused, he would perform one of his Dooley Deeds. It was incredible to see how many kids were actually sucked into doing one of Dirk's Dares. He would laugh right in your face and make sure all the kids at school found out about it when you actually did one of his dares. Most kids who did the Dooley Dares were just afraid of what would happen if they didn't do what Dirk wanted.

It was a cold November morning when Arlie arrived at Finkle. Arlie was a new student who was from a small community just outside Paris, France. Everyone thought Arlie dressed funny and talked really weird, at least a lot differently than the other kids at Milmac Public. Arlie was a boy who tried hard to fit in. He wanted to be cool, but always ended up saying or doing the wrong things. He heard about the famous Dooley Dares. He thought that if he could do a "Dooley" he could gain the cool reputation he was desperately seeking. He thought it was his only chance.

Dirk was at the back of the playground harassing the younger kids. He was giving a boy a wicked wedgie. He wanted the boy's lunch money.

"Hey, are you the famous Dirk Dooley?" asked Arlie.

"Who wants to know?" yelled Dirk.

"I just heard that you were the coolest guy in school. I really want to hang out with you and your gang."

Arlie thought that he would have a better chance of joining Dirk and his gang if he laid it on thick with flattering words. He wanted to join in so badly that he was willing to do anything in order to prove himself worthy.

Dirk could not believe his ears. It was going to be so easy to make Arlie look like a fool. You see, Dirk never intended on being Arlie's friend. All he wanted to do was to control and embarrass Arlie. He was going to get Arlie to do the ultimate Dooley Dare.

Dirk thought for a good five minutes. This was a record for Dirk. He finally came up with the ultimate Dooley.

"Let's see how brave you really are, Arlie. If you want to hang around with my friends and me, you have to prove that you are not a wimp. You have to walk up to the top of Screaming Hill and enter the grounds of the Hangman's Tower. Then, you must climb to the top of Hangman's Tower and grab something from one of the three rooms you will find there. This will prove that you were actually in the tower."

Hangman's Tower was where Civil War soldiers from Fort Guthery were tortured and hung by the neck for crimes they were accused of during the war. The legend says that every evening around midnight you can hear the moans, screams and the snapping of the necks of the tortured souls who met their end there. All the kids at Finkle knew the stories about Hangman's Tower, but Arlie did not.

He thought for a minute while Dirk waited in anticipation. Arlie wanted to be popular, to have a friend, so he agreed to Dirk's Dooley Dare.

It was a cold, bone-chilling night. The moon was bright in the sky and seemed bigger than it had been all year. It was so cold that you could see your breath freeze in the air. The wind was howling through the rotting boards that entombed the sleeping souls of the town. Arlie put on his warmest jacket and began his climb up Screaming Hill. Dirk was waiting for him at the path entrance that lead up to Hangman's Tower. As Arlie approached Dirk, he noticed that this over-grown bully was standing in front of something. Unknown to Arlie it was a sign that read, "No Trespassing - Danger - Keep Out!"

"Are you sure it is safe to go into the tower" asked Arlie.

"Of course," Dirk replied, "You're not starting to chicken out are you? I knew you weren't cool enough to be part of my group!" he taunted.

"I'm the coolest guy you will ever meet and I am going to prove it!" replied Arlie.

Arlie began his walk up the winding path, which seemed to engulf his entire body in its darkness. He could hear the sounds of the night getting louder as he approached the tower. All of a sudden... silence. The night sounds stopped. Arlie approached the black iron gate and opened it. The gate creaked open with a spine-chilling wail that sent a shiver up Arlie's back. His heart beat faster as he made his way along the stone path that led toward Hangman's Tower. As he crept closer to the tower door, he got the feeling that he was being watched. Were the souls of the dead awake and waiting? Arlie began to tremble as he slowly pushed the old, wooden door open. He could see a spiral, stone staircase, which must lead to the three rooms, which Dirk had told him about.

"I cannot believe I am actually doing this!" thought Arlie. "Is this really what it takes to prove you are cool?"

Arlie slowly climbed the stairs. He was stepping over the remains of decomposing rats, which lined the steps.

"I can hardly see!" exclaimed Arlie. "I just know I am going to find myself face to face with some ghost. I just have this feeling!"

Finally, after what seemed to be an eternity, Arlie reached the hallway that held the secrets of the three rooms.

"OK, all I have to do is go into one of these rooms, grab an object and hand it over to Dirk. How hard can that be?"

Arlie didn't want to waste any time so he quickly moved toward the first door. It took all of his strength to push open this decaying door only to see that the room was empty. Arlie could not believe his eyes.

"Empty! How could this room be empty? Dirk told me that every room was filled with old soldier's gear? How can I prove that I am cool if I don't have anything to show I actually was in Hangman's Tower?"

Was this one of Dirk Dooley's tricks? Arlie tried the second door. This room was empty, too! Arlie sat down with his back against the third door. A tear rolled down his face. All he wanted was to be cool. This was exactly what had happened in his old school in France. Kids would make him do the stupidest things in order to prove himself. He ended up being teased more because of being dumb enough to do the dare. Was this going to happen again?

Arlie started to smell a very strange, but familiar odor. It rather smelled like his brother Declan's room after a visit to his favorite Mexican Burrito joint. All of a sudden, there was a thud and a loud groan. Someone was in the locked room, but who? Arlie began to beat against the door. He demanded that the person behind the door show himself.

"Unlock the door!" Arlie shouted.

Booming from behind the rotted door came a voice with a strong Scottish accent.

"For goodness sake… I'm trying to go to the toilet. Do ye mind?"

What was this? Someone was going to the washroom in Hangman's Tower? Arlie banged again. This time even louder.

"Come out of there and show yourself!" demanded Arlie. "This is not a public washroom, you know!"

This time the strange voice echoed in an even stronger Scottish accent.

"For goodness sake... plhhp... oh, look what you made me do! My new pants are ruined!"

Arlie gave the door a swift kick with his foot and a bump with his backside, pushing the door wide open. Inside, to his surprise was an empty room. There definitely was a funky smell happening, but no sign of anyone. From down the hall, Arlie heard footsteps running frantically down the stone spiral staircase and out into the backyard. Another door was opened and slammed shut. Who was this guy? A toilet troll? Stinky Sam? Poopy Patinski? Arlie had heard of Poopy and Stinky before he ever got to Finkle. Could the stories he heard about them be true?

Arlie ran down the stairs and into the backyard where he saw what looked to be an old outside toilet. He heard they were commonly called Johnny-on-the-Spot or Kybos. One name that Arlie heard that he thought funny was Thunder-Box, a name often used to describe any outhouse used by his brother Declan. As Arlie approached the outhouse, he noticed the same funky smell. Again, he banged on the door of the outhouse and demanded that the person show himself. For the third and final time the voice screamed out.

"Can't a boy be left alone... I'm trying to take a poop... do ye mind?"

All of a sudden, the door burst open, revealing a short boy, dressed in old brown shorts, and a tartan shirt. He was racing around the yard pulling his pants up from around his ankles. The one obvious thing that Arlie noticed about this boy was that he was transparent. You could actually see right through him. Was this the famous ghost of a Civil War soldier or just a ghost of the toilet? Arlie wasn't scared because who would be afraid of a ghost who hung around a toilet?

"You are the first person who has seen me who has not run away screaming GHOST!" exclaimed the ghost. "I am Reaky Bye-Bye and I roam the grounds of Hangman's Tower. I can not leave this place until I tell my story and befriend someone of this world. Will you listen to my story, Arlie?"

Arlie was shocked. How did this ghost know his name and what was his story going to be about? Arlie agreed to listen. They both sat under an eerie elm tree as Reaky Bye-Bye began to tell the story of how he became a ghost.

"It began on an ordinary June day. I, Reaky Bye-Bye, was playing Hide-and- Go-Seek with my sister. She could find me no matter where I hid. I decided to hide somewhere upstairs. I heard her coming up the stairs so I had to think fast. I was in the bathroom so I thought I could hide in the shower. I knew she probably would turn on the shower and soak me so I thought maybe the clothes hamper? An image of my Dad's dirty underwear and socks popped into my mind! Forget that! I had to think quickly. Where was I to hide? I saw the toilet behind me. As you can see, I am kind of a small guy so I

took the plunge, in a manner of speaking. I placed my bottom in the toilet and crouched down, lowering the toilet lid over my head. She would never find me here, or so I thought! I heard my sister enter the bathroom. The first thing she did was turn on the shower. She thought for sure she could soak me, but she was soon disappointed to see I hadn't hidden there. She then rifled through the laundry bin. Dirty underwear and socks were flying everywhere. My cat Fluffy got hit with a flying pair of underwear. We never saw her again. We think she may have developed a Gotchiphobia… the fear of flying underwear.

My sister called out, "I know you're in here, you little rug rat. Get out from under those dirty boxers."

When I didn't reply she began to heave the underwear and socks all over the bathroom. She emptied the bin in only a few seconds. I thought I had finally fooled my sister when everything all of a sudden took a turn for the worse. She walked slowly toward the toilet. She turned around and sat right down on the lid. I could see her legs dangling in front of me. Then, I heard the most evil laugh I had ever heard in my entire life. She slowly turned around and FLUSHED ME DOWN THE TOILET! I was twirling and swirling down the long pipes that ran through and beneath our house. It was the longest and smelliest ride of my life. Finally, I arrived at my destination. It was dark, damp and wet and boy did it smell! I realized that I had ended up in the outside toilet. How in the world was I going to get out of this mess? I looked up through the toilet seat hole and noticed that the outhouse was beginning to sway back and forth. There were loud bangs and clatters coming from above. The wind was howling through the rotten bits of board that held the outhouse together. Then, I heard a sound that almost made my heart skip a beat. It sounded like a train engine barreling down the tracks. I remembered hearing a weather watch warning about a tornado that could be coming this way. I had heard that when a tornado is near it sounds like a train engine. Before I could come up with a plan the tornado rolled over the outhouse, blasting me and it's remains into outer space.

Now the only way I can move onto the Great Beyond is if I can make an earthly friend. To be honest with you, I was not much of a friend to any one when I was alive. I would promise my friendship to the kids in my class, but only if they did one of my dares. I wasn't really interested in being their friend. I just enjoyed the feeling of power I got when I got someone to do something stupid. It's probably the same feeling my sister got when she picked on me. It's not that I didn't want friends. I didn't think anyone would actually like me. I tried to be cool by using my age and my intelligence to pick on kids younger and smaller than I was. I mean, I was small for my age, so I had to pick on younger kids.

Arlie thought for a moment and realized that Dirk Dooley was doing exactly the same thing this Reaky Bye-Bye was doing.

"He didn't want to be my friend. He was just trying to control me." sighed Arlie.

"I would be happy to be your friend, Reaky. You seem like a cool guy. Maybe we can hang out and tell each other stories. Do you know any ghost stories? Oops... of course you do... you are a ghost after all."

Reaky couldn't believe his ears. Someone actually wanted to be his friend and he didn't have to do anything to prove himself.

Arlie and Reaky shook hands and agreed to meet each other every Saturday to exchange cool stories. Arlie was really looking forward to Reaky's ghost stories, because who better to tell a spooky story than a spook himself!

Arlie ran down the hill with a roll of toilet paper flying in the breeze. He stopped at the main gate where Dirk Dooley was waiting. Arlie flung the toilet roll at Dirk, pinging him in the head.

"Hey, where do you think you are going, small fry? Don't you want to be part of my gang?" Dirk demanded.

"I realize now that you don't have to prove anything to anybody. If someone wants to be your friend, they will accept you for who you are. You do not have to do any silly Dooley Dare to prove yourself. Anyway, I don't think you're very cool. I realize now that people who dare you want to control you and set you up to do nasty things. True friends help and listen to each other, and grow together. My new friend Reaky is cool because he likes me for who I am. So, see ya. Wouldn't want to be ya!"

Arlie fulfilled his promise and met with Reaky every Saturday. They grew into great friends. They shared good, bad, happy and sad times, and as each day passed, their friendship grew. In fact, although Reaky had fulfilled the requirements of making an earthly friend, he decided to remain a ghost at Hangman's Tower in order to keep his friendship with Arlie.

AMAZON VACATION

Chapter 7

The Boogaloo family lo-o-ov-ed going on vacation. They didn't just go to Florida or to a cottage. They went to EXOTIC places. They'd been on a safari in Africa, sailed the Caribbean Sea, climbed Mount Everest and had even been to see the pyramids of Egypt. They loved adventure!

One sunny Saturday morning, Mr. and Mrs. Boogaloo were bursting with some exciting news.

"Where is everyone?" they yelled as they pushed their slightly rotund bodies through the narrow kitchen doorway.

"We have planned an adventure this family will never forget! We're going to a place that is hot, exotic and full of adventure. We're going to... the Amazon!"

Binky and Hannah, son and daughter of Mr. and Mrs. Boogaloo, couldn't believe their ears. The Amazon? Aa-mazing! They had never been to the Amazon before... but... what was an Amazon?

"The Amazon is a river in South America," explained Mr. Boogaloo. "It is one of the longest rivers in the entire world. Along the Amazon

River you will experience life as you have never experienced it before! There are groups of people who look different than the people of Finkle. These tribesmen place large wooden dishes in their mouths, which extend their lips about six inches from their faces."

"I bet you could get one heck of a kiss from those guys!" remarked Mrs. Boogaloo.

"And there are headhunters who collect the heads of unsuspecting tourists. They boil them until they are small enough to wear as jewelry. And let's not forget about the anaconda snakes that hang about in the trees waiting for a chance to crush your bones into dust. Spiders, scorpions, and all sorts of creepy crawly things are there to keep everyone amused," continued Mr. Boogaloo. "What more could you ask for?"

The Boogaloo family just stood there looking at each other.

"Well," asked the father, "What are you waiting for? Let's get packed!!"

As if the seats of their pants were on fire, each member of the Boogaloo family took off to their rooms, grabbed their suitcases and began packing. Shorts, T-shirts, hiking boots, running shoes, mosquito repellent, and extra pairs of underwear were all crammed into their suitcases. Extra pairs of underwear were always a necessity as the potential for "scary moments" was always a great risk on a Boogaloo adventure. The Boogaloo's were ready for the most memorable time of their lives.

No one could sleep very well that night as the excitement about going on an Amazon vacation filled their minds with the possibilities of battling crocodiles, swimming with piranhas and coming face to face with an Amazon tribesman.

"Amazon, here we come!"

Early the next morning, long before the sun had even clipped the horizon, the Boogaloo family loaded their belongings into the family van and headed for the airport. When they arrived at the airport they unloaded all their baggage, parked the van and trudged through a sea of people to their airline's flight desk. They were excited to be flying on the maiden voyage of Crash and Burn Airlines. The Boogaloos loaded their baggage onto the scales and handed the attendant their tickets. Mr. Boogaloo noticed the attendant's badge which indicated that this was actually the pilot of Crash and Burn Airlines. It was Captain Crash himself! His coke-bottle glasses and his inability to speak English made Mr. Boogaloo a little nervous, but not beyond what he could handle. The seeing-eye dog and a book entitled, "How to Fly a Plane Without an Engine" were a little much, but still not enough to make the Boogaloos turn back from this adventure. Captain Crash handed back their tickets, shuffled their baggage onto the belt and asked the family if they had any next of kin to notify in case of emergency. This was definitely going to be an adventure the Boogaloos would not soon forget!

It takes a long time to get to the Amazon. Binky Boogaloo, the youngest of the Boogaloo family, filled five barf bags before the plane even left the ground. He was a little nervous. The Boogaloos had to change planes six times. Each time they changed planes, the plane got smaller. They were finally on the last leg of their trip and flying in a small six-seater Cessna. Soon they would be arriving at their final destination.

They stared out the tiny windows of the plane as the hills and valleys of the Brazilian countryside passed beneath them.

"This is going to be a great vacation!" sighed Mrs. Boogaloo.

"Bwwwp. Bwwwp."

"That didn't sound like the plane," thought the father. "It sounds as if it's coming from inside the plane."

It wasn't long before the plane filled with a smell like no other smell. It was even worse than old Aunt Bunny's stinky toes. It smelled as if it was coming from the deepest and darkest parts of the human body. You see, the night before the Boogaloo family mistakenly treated themselves to some South American home cooking. They weren't used to such spicy food and now they were paying for indulging themselves. The smell was almost unbearable. The pilot could barely see, as his eyes were burning and filling with tears. Breathing was impossible. The pilot managed to safely land the plane in the deepest part of the Amazon rainforest. Animals were dropping out of the trees as the smell travelled around the plane's surroundings.

The Boogaloos had reached their destination. They were nestled deep in the heart of the Rainforest. The only way of travelling from this point was by donkey. So they loaded their backpacks and supplies onto their donkeys, secured proper maps of the area, and started on their Amazon vacation.

The Boogaloos travelled into the darkest and most secluded areas of the rainforest. They were amazed and awestruck at the variety of animals, reptiles, and birds they were able to see. Mr. Boogaloo had arranged to meet their tour guide by nightfall. The travel agent told him that this was the best guide they had. His name was Inka of the Yu-Yu Tribe. He stood six foot eight inches tall and had the look of a warrior. His face was painted with the colors of the forest. Inka knew everything about every animal, every tree and every untouched area of the Amazon River. He

also knew of the tremendous dangers that could await unprepared tourists.

The only problem with Inka was understanding him. The only language he spoke was that of the Yu-Yu Tribe. The only thing he ever seemed to say was "Buga, Buga, Bugaboo!" in a high pitched squeal!

They could say, "How are you today Inka?"and would hear "Buga, Buga, Bugaboo," or Binky would joke, "Can we feed you to the anaconda?" and again they would hear, "Buga, Buga, Bugaboo."

Inka was a pretty cool guy, just hard to understand. He was pretty good at hand signals too. He motioned with his giant hands that the Boogaloo family was to load their gear onto the raft. Once that was done, Inka pushed off from shore so that the Amazon Adventure could begin.

The family saw many strange and wonderful creatures. There were brightly coloured dart frogs, deadly spiders and monkeys chattering in the trees. They even saw a giant anaconda swimming in the water... that was really freaky... the snake was massive!

Inka taught the Boogaloo family the importance of living together as one. All of the different animals of the rain forest lived together in peace and harmony. There was the usual battle for survival, but there was no unnecessary violence. It was almost as if the animals and various tribes of the rainforest respected each other's differences and celebrated them. It was cool! After all, you never see leopards being made fun of because of their spots or the elephants being teased because of their long trunks. Humans should learn from the animals.

The group had been travelling down the Amazon River for almost a week when it happened! Inka went ballistic! He starting screaming and waving his gangly arms above his head.

"Buga, Buga, Bugaboo! Buga, Buga, Bugaboo!" yelled Inka.

"What in the world does that mean?" asked Mrs. Boogaloo.

"Maybe he's caught a bad case of Mi-lu Fever. They say it can drive a person crazy." stated Mr. Boogaloo.

Without warning, Inka jumped off the raft and swam to shore. He disappeared into the rainforest leaving behind a bewildered Boogaloo family.

What in the world had happened ? What did Inka see that terrified him so much?

The only thing the Boogaloos knew for sure was that Inka did a stinka! The smell he left behind reminded them of the horrendous plane flight. Wow! What a stink! The Boogaloos were in shock as they continued to float down the river. They had no idea what was coming, but they knew that the sound they heard was that of danger.

The family looked in the direction of the rushing water and realized that they were heading towards a waterfall. Mr. Boogaloo looked on his map and realized they were heading towards Devil's Elbow! They had to think fast! Anything that sailed over Devil's Elbow would be splinterized, especially human bone.

Mr. Boogaloo started throwing their supplies overboard and the kids joined in. The mother grabbed the steering oar and tried her best to steer them towards shore, but even with a lighter raft they were being pulled towards Devil's Elbow. The only thing they could do was jump overboard and swim for shore and hope that they would be strong enough to reach the safety of the shoreline before tumbling over the falls. With a "heave ho and away we go!" the Boogaloos jumped. The raft shot past them. It tumbled down Devil's Elbow and shattered on the rocks below. Was the Boogaloo family destined for the same fate? Luckily for them a storm the night before had brought down a tree into the river. The tree trunk stretched across the river. They had to swim for the tree. It was their only hope.

Mr. Boogaloo yelled, "Grab hold of each other. We'll make a chain and pull ourselves toward the tree trunk!"

Struggling against the current the family was able to grab the branches of the tree and pull themselves up onto the safety of the trunk. Team work paid off again. If it wasn't for the fact that the family worked together to solve their problem they would not have survived. They had used so much energy just getting out of the river that when they had reached the safety of the shore, they lay back to rest. They slept through the night to the break of day.

When they awoke the next morning it was to a blood curdling scream! The scream was coming from one of them! Mr. and Mrs. Boogaloo and Binky's sister Hannah all looked at each other and then at Binky. His eyes were wide with terror! There on his chest was a Jube-Jube spider. A Jube-Jube spider is so sensitive that if you even make the slightest movement it will scratch you with its leg spikes and a highly potent poison will enter through your skin. Within five minutes you would be dead! They all froze! No one knew what to do, but before they could even think about a solution, the father looked up to find they were surrounded in the trees by this really funky looking Indian tribe. The Indians had really weird mambo lips, bones

in their noses, and strategically placed loincloths. One of the Indians was dressed slightly differently. Mr. Boogaloo assumed this must be the chief of the tribe. This tribesman had a long pole with what looked like a scoop on one end. Carefully straddling a branch right above Binky, the Indian chief swung his pole, scooped down, right across the boy's chest. The Jube-Jube Spider was picked up in one swift movement! The spider was then flung across the river and found itself SPLAT on the other side on top of a log. The family watched the spider's flight and turned to thank the tribe for their help, only to find that the tribe had disappeared! Vooosh! Gone! Without even a sound they had disappeared as quickly as they had appeared.

After surviving in the rainforest for several days the Boogaloo family was rescued by another tourist company. The family was able to purchase a few new items of clothing and they continued their interrupted vacation with no other serious misfortunes.

Upon returning to their home in Canada, the family took a trip to the library to look up information on the Jube-Jube spider. They found out that it was known to be the most poisonous spider in all of the rainforest, with a bite that could kill you within five minutes. What the spider was also known for was scratching its host with its hind legs and laying its eggs in the wound. A person would think that it was just a little scratch, until a few weeks later the small Jube-Jube spiders would hatch. Poison would be released from the hatchlings, killing its host immediately! This could have happened to Binky if the Ghost Tribe had not come to his rescue. But, where had they come from? Why did they help the family who were foreigners to their land? The family hadn't even had a chance to say thank you.

The Boogaloos failed to find any information on the Ghost Tribe in their library search. However, a few nights later on a TV show called Mysteries of the World, there was a special feature about Ghost Tribes. Of particular interest to the family was a segment on Ghost Tribes of the Amazon. The narrator began talking about a specific Ghost Tribe that would help people who were in trouble. They had saved over twenty families so far. They would help these families, and as quickly as they appeared, would disappear. The only facts that could be passed along were the experiences of those people who had been directly affected by the Ghost Tribe - those they had helped in some way.

Binky could not understand why this tribe had helped him out. They didn't receive money, food or even a thank you. Most of the time the people they helped were foreigners. They certainly weren't friends.

On his way to school, Binky was thinking about how this Ghost Tribe saved his life for no apparent reason. He was riding his bike and was lost in his thoughts when he rounded a corner and SMASH! He ran right into Mrs. Stinkle from down the street. Old Mrs. Stinkle went butt-surfing one way as Binky flew off his bike the other. Poor Mrs. Stinkle, who must be at least 85, was trying to struggle to her feet when Binky came running up to her.

"I'm so sorry, Mrs. Stinkle. Are you all right?"

He felt so badly and began picking up Mrs. Stinkle's spilled groceries and putting them back in her basket.

"I really am sorry, Mrs. Stinkle. Please let me help you by carrying your groceries home for you," he said earnestly.

"I'm fine, I'm fine." said Mrs. Stinkle. "I would appreciate your help carrying my groceries home. I feel a little woozy."

"No problem. It's the least I can do."

Mrs. Stinkle was concerned for Binky as well. She wanted to make sure that he was okay. He shook off her concern by stating that he was fine. He carried the groceries all the way to her house, up the front steps and into the kitchen.

"Thank you very much, Binky. Most children would have taken off after the accident and not cared. You are an amazing little boy!"

He felt really good because even though he had made a mistake, his kindness and thoughtfulness had helped someone else out. He felt really great inside!

It occurred to him all at once what the Ghost Tribe got out of helping people! It wasn't for money, or material things; it was for the feeling it gave them when they had helped someone out. You couldn't put a price tag on it, because it wasn't for sale... it was something you earned by doing. It was given to you free of charge! A sense of self-worth and feeling good within yourself that you had done something for someone else just because they needed your help. That was worth more than his allowance or his birthday money. Binky felt as if he had a new energy and power within himself. He was confident he could do anything. If he put his mind to doing it, it could be done.

Mrs. Stinkle offered Binky some cookies and a glass of milk and asked if he would be interested in cutting her grass. He came back every week for the next five years to do Mrs. Stinkle's lawn. She paid him when she could, but most of the time he just asked for cookies and milk and a chance to talk to her. She turned out to be a really interesting lady with tons of stories about places she had visited as a stewardess on a cruise line. Binky loved spending time just listening to Mrs. Stinkle. He never realized how interesting old people could be and how many lessons you could learn.

SWAMP CAMPING

Chapter 8

Mojo was a big boy for his age. He stood six foot two and weighed close to two hundred pounds. He had spikey blond hair and wore the baggiest pants you have ever seen. He was known as "the friendly giant" by the boys in his grade four class at Milmac Public School. The truth was that Mojo should have been in grade six, but was held back because of his inability to read. No one dared to make fun of Mojo. Not directly to his face anyways.

The one thing Mojo was known for, other than his size, was his camping adventures. Mojo loved camping! He loved camping so much that he camped out every night. Other kids knew that Mojo would camp anywhere. He had camped up in a tree once. He almost broke his head when he fell out in the middle of the night and landed on it. He squished a poor, helpless squirrel flat, who was innocently collecting nuts under the big oak. That squirrel was never the same!

The most bizarre place Mojo camped was on a raft down in the Bayou. An alligator plum near bit Mojo's toes right off. If it wasn't for the smell of those toes, Mojo was sure to be a gonner.

Mojo had quite the reputation and no one in their right mind would go camping with him.

It was a Monday afternoon and the luckiest day of Mojo's life. It was when Stanley B. Stoople came to town. He was about the same age as Mojo, but not quite as smart. That's not being too complimentary, as Mojo was no genius. Mojo and Stanley became the best of friends. They did everything together. Mojo finally had someone he could go camping with. Mojo really liked Stanley as Stanley was someone who liked him for who he was. He didn't have to pretend to be someone he was not. He didn't have to be the class-clown or the schoolyard bully. Mojo just had to be himself because this was all that Stanley expected.

Both Mojo and Stanley had heard that there was a swamp about five miles along the shoreline from where they lived. This swamp was believed to be a place of doom and evil. It was well known that you could go in, but you would never come out! Now they were not really sure if they should believe any of the stories that they had heard, so they decided that the best way to find out was to go camping there.

Early Saturday morning, the boys set out along the shoreline. It started off as a beautiful day, but quickly turned into the coldest and darkest day of the summer. As they slowly made their way along the beach they noticed old, weathered signs that were slowly decomposing from the fierce sea winds and rugged waves that bashed their fragile frames. These signs had skulls and crossbones etched onto their surfaces.

They read, "Beware… Danger… Go Back Before it's Too Late… "

These words of warning did not stop Mojo or Stanley from entering the darkest entrance they had ever seen. The entrance led into the swamp.

"Do you really think we should go in? It looks kind of dangerous." murmured Stanley.

"Oh, don't be such a chicken," snapped Mojo. "There's nothing to worry about. It will be an adventure!"

As they entered the swamp its blackness engulfed them. It was so dark they could barely see two feet in front of them. They stumbled over rocks and roots until they reached the spot where they decided to make camp. They set up under an old oak tree which provided shelter from the cold rain and the winds which were piercing their bones like jagged swords. As the wind howled through the trees, both Stanley and Mojo set up their tent and prepared their camp site for a night in the swamp. They made a fire pit and lit a fire, using the small kindling and branches that they had found near the oak tree.

They each found a place to sit, and began telling ghost stories about the swamp. There was a legend told in their community about a hermit who used to live in the swamp. He was known to prey upon innocent children. When the campfire embers were aglow and darkness fell upon a campsite, the hermit would take his sleeping victims away from their restful sleeps. They would never be seen again.

Mojo and Stanley were scaring each other with these stories of the hermit. Mojo almost wet his pants when an owl let out a blood-curdling screech. He was spinning in circles for at least five minutes.

They didn't know what time it was, but knew it must be dark beyond the boundaries of the swamp, because they were getting a little tired. They crept into their tent, got into their sleeping bags, told each other a few jokes and quickly fell asleep. It was about two hours later when they were awakened by a noise coming from the swamp! It didn't sound like anything they had ever heard before!

"What was that? asked Stanley. "Do you think it is some wild creature looking for food?"

"I don't know. Let's go check it out!" whispered Mojo.

They struggled out of their sleeping bags and cautiously opened the tent flap, popping their heads out of the tent to see what was making the strange noise. Mojo grabbed his flashlight and dragged Stanley out of the tent by his underwear to check out the area of the swamp where they thought the noise had come from. Not far from their campsite, in fact frighteningly close, was the swamp with an eerie stillness and layer of green slime which lay motionless on the top. The boys couldn't believe their eyes when they saw something swimming around in the water... something that looked like it had a fin! They both knew that there wasn't supposed to be anything living in the swamp, so what was it that was swimming in circles?

Mojo had a great idea! He went back to the tent and grabbed his fishing net.

"Stand near the edge of the water. When the creature comes to the surface bop it on the head. I will scoop it up in the fishing net," he commanded Stanley.

Mojo thought it would be really cool to capture the creature and take it to school to scare all the girls and his teacher Mrs. Finklestein. Just think... Mrs. Finklestein would walk to the front of the class as she usually did, greet the class and casually open the top drawer to her desk to retrieve her pointer stick. Instead of grabbing onto a long, wooden pointer stick, she would be grabbing onto a slimy, scaley, two eyed swamp creature. She would freak! Her eyes would bug out and her head would start spinning! It was a prank no grade four kid could resist.

Mojo and Stanley both agreed to put the plan into action. They went to the edge of the water to wait for the creature to surface again. They had waited for about an hour, when all of a sudden they saw the creature. It was heading straight for the shore. As it got closer to the boys it slowed down. It was as if it was slowing down to check them out. It stopped right at the feet of Mojo who was patiently waiting with his flashlight. Mojo reached over his head and was about to bop this swamp creature on the head when it shot out of the water. It grabbed onto Mojo and pulled him into the darkness of the swamp. Stanley did not know what to do!

"Mojo! Mojo! Where in the world did you go?"

Stanley didn't know if he should stay or if he should run for help.

"I think I've peed my pants!"screamed Stanley.

Stanley had never been so scared as he was in that moment. From beneath the blackened depths of the swamp popped Mojo's boxers.

"Barney boxers!" screamed Stanley. "You've got to be kidding! I hope they belong to the creature, Mojo! The kids at school would never let you live that one down!"

Stanley was so scared that his knees crashed together as his whole body shook! He thought about running, but his legs wouldn't move. Before he had a chance to think again about running away, the creature surfaced right in front of him and jumped up from the water, pulling him under the slime and down to the bottom of the swamp!

After what seemed like forever, Stanley emerged in an underwater cave! There, sitting shivering on a rock, was Mojo! They sat beside each other shaking from the cold and from being wet. The cave was very dark and filled with spiders and rats. It smelled really gross, like Mojo's room after he had baked beans for dinner! They looked across the cave only to see a figure staring back at them. This creature almost looked human. Its body looked human, but its face looked as if it had been transformed into a hideous monster. Actually, the creature looked like a pretty version of Mojo's Aunt Bunny. She was a woman who could give any boy a good nightmare.

The creature motioned to Mojo and Stanley to follow it. What choice did they have? They got up and followed it down a long narrow path, which led deeper and deeper into the bowels of the earth. It was getting darker and colder as the boys followed this strange being through the endless tunnels and catacombs that led to who knows where. They wondered where they were going and what awaited them once they got to the end of the path. Was there an underground village of these swamp creatures? Were they going to their death? Were they dinner?

After what seemed like miles, Mojo and Stanley rounded a corner and stood in the biggest room they had ever seen. It was at least five football fields in length and in the room was gold! Mounds and mounds of gold doubloons, rubies, emeralds, sapphires and diamonds! But, most amazing of all was what filled the center of the room. It was a pirate ship!

The boys looked at each other and both blurted out at the same time, "A Spanish galleon!"

They could see an image of a skull and cross bones embroidered on the tattered flag that once was flying on the mast of this mighty ship. The sight of this flag would have put fear into the heart and mind of the bravest man. On the side of the ship was the name 'Captain Blair'.

Mojo had heard about Captain Blair in Mrs. Finklestein's class. The legend was that Captain Blair was an old sea pirate who had sailed around to different ports and taken treasure from any town that he happened to sail into! The boys knew, however, from their history books, that Captain Blair was alive in the 1600's! It was said that Captain Blair had encountered a storm one night as he slept. It had been such a violent

storm that his ship was swallowed by an avenging sea. The Captain and his crew were presumed dead, as they were never seen again.

What had really happened was that Captain Blair's ship had been blown into this cave which originally had been at the sea's edge. The storm had caused a landslide that covered the entrance to the cave! As the sea made new avenues and rivers into the mainland, the ship, the crew and the treasure had been encapsulated in the swamp!

"That means the treasure belongs to us, if we can only get it out of here," screamed Mojo.

They climbed aboard the ship and were jumping in piles of doubloons when Stanley slipped and slid down the mound of gold into the arms of Captain Blair himself... or what was left of him! Stanley struggled and screamed as he tried to get the skeleton's arms from around his waist! Finally he broke free and both boys climbed as fast as they could to the floor of the cave from which they had come.

At first, Mojo and Stanley were really excited about finding all the treasure, but they soon realized that if Captain Blair and his crew had not been able to find a way out of the cave, neither would they! The boys sat on a pile of gold on the cave floor, surrounded by Captain Blair and his skeleton crew and tried to figure out a way to get out of the cave. They had almost forgotten about the swamp creature when they heard a flapping above their heads. Thinking that it was the creature, they looked up quickly, just in time to see a rare, African Moo-

Moo Chicken flying into a hole in the cave wall, very high up, close to the roof of the cave!

"There must be a way in and out if there is a Moo-Moo Chicken in the cave!" screamed Stanley.

"Just keep your eye on the bird, Mojo. We'll wait to see where the Moo-Moo Chicken got in and that will be our way out!"

They waited patiently until the bird re-entered the cave. As the Moo-Moo Chicken flew over Mojo it released a huge load of poop. Unfortunately, Mojo's mouth was open as the bird's load was released. It went straight past Mojo's lips, through his mouth and into his stomach.

"It tastes like chicken, said Mojo. "Kind of sweet and sour."

Mojo and Stanley climbed up the steep wall of the cave. They helped each other scale the slippery surface of the cave wall. As they reached the top of the cave they saw a narrow tunnel that shot upwards toward the surface. They used both their arms and legs pressed against the sides of the tunnel to climb up and out of the cave. They were being scratched by the roots which filled the tunnel, not to mention the earwigs, worms and snails that were finding their way into the ears and nostrils of both boys.

To their surprise, Mojo and Stanley came up right beside the old oak tree! Their campsite was right on the other side of the tree. Now the boys knew a way in, and a way out of the cave! The treasure was theirs!

They promised each other never to tell anyone where the treasure was. They slid down into the cave, filled their knap sacks with as much gold as they could carry, and headed off for their homes. The one thing that plagued their minds was the creature. They didn't believe in monsters, but how could they deny what they saw? It was a true mystery as to where the creature had come from. Was it the ghost of one of the pirates, or maybe an unidentified creature? Why did this creature show them the treasure, then disappear? Mojo and Stanley needed to figure out what, exactly they had seen in the swamp. They needed to solve the mystery that lurked behind this swamp creature.

They headed to town to visit the library. For hours, they looked through old newspapers and books on the history of the swamp. They finally came across an article about a scientist by the name of Bill Haddock. He was a strange sort of man who was interested in changing the swamp into a livable area. Some say that something went wrong with one of his experiments, transforming his appearance, into what looked like a swamp creature. Bill tried to live as he normally did in the community, but because of his deformed appearance, he was teased and bullied, till he was driven into the swamp. He was never seen again.

Bill Haddock must have discovered Captain Blair's treasure during his time in the swamp. He must have wanted to show someone where the treasure was before he disappeared forever. He had picked Mojo and Stanley because he saw how they treated each other with respect. They acknowledged each other's differences and celebrated them. Both Stanley and Mojo learned that being different was cool. They also had the courage to come into the swamp and experience all that it had to offer. Bill admired their courage and their ability to accept each other for who they were, faults and all.

Mojo and Stanley left the library with a new understanding about the importance of celebrating differences. The boys wanted to go back and help Bill, and at least thank him for all he had given to them, but they didn't find a trace of him after that day. The boys looked for weeks in different areas of the swamp but never found anything to suggest that the scientist had ever been there at all.

Mojo and Stanley grew up to be the richest members of their community, never telling anyone about the treasure that lay beneath the swamp. They were followed numerous times into the swamp but no one could ever keep up with them. Time and time again they were asked where all their money came from, but they never gave up their secret. They didn't want hundreds of money-hungry people scrounging through the swamp and destroying it, especially if Bill was still alive. They wanted to make sure that Bill was able to live in peace and not be ridiculed by a society which was intolerant to individuals who are different.

Mojo wrote a speech which he presented to his class on being different. He found it sad that the world totally ignores, humiliates and ostracizes people who are different, whether it's because of a physical difference or a personality difference. The key to being happy is to accept yourself as you are because everyone has something to offer. Mojo and Stanley knew that being different was alright and it was time to celebrate differences and from that day that is what they did.

AVEY YO-YO

Chapter 9

(Folk Tale, Adapted by Scott Graham)

"Calm down, Tommy. We know you are excited, but you need to get a grip. You have been driving everyone crazy for the last week. For goodness sake, it's just another birthday!" exclaimed Doris, Tommy's older sister.

Doris picked up the heaviest book she could find and heaved it at Tommy's head. He ducked just as the book sailed past him, landing on his pet hamster, Petey. The hamster was a little worse for wear, but managed to survive the incident.

"We can call Petey, Pancake Pete," laughed Tommy.

Doris began to scream, "Mo-o-om! Tommy's bugging me!"

She wanted him out of her room and as far away as possible. It worked. Tommy zipped down the stairs and flew into the kitchen. He was in search of his birthday present.

It was Tommy's tenth birthday. It was the day when he would move from a single digit to a double digit. Tommy was going to have a party with his friends, who would bring a truckload of presents. He would also be eating mounds of ice cream and cake. His mom always made Chocolate Fudge Brownie Supreme for his birthday. One bite of it would shoot the quietest kid into an energized frenzy for a week. Not that Tommy had a problem being energized - he was a boy in constant motion. You could bribe him with a million dollars and he still would be unable to sit still.

Tommy had been asking for a video game player for his birthday for as long as he could remember. His parents did not approve of video games. They felt it taught children inappropriate ways of handling their problems. Still, Tommy hoped that his parents would give in and buy him the video player anyway.

He frantically looked around the kitchen for his present. There it was! Sitting on the kitchen table was a huge, brightly decorated box. Tommy knew it had to be the video game player. It just had to be! Tommy ripped open the paper and was into the box in a matter of seconds. There inside the box was a... .guitar?

"A guitar?" moaned Tommy, "What on earth am I going to do with a guitar? I don't know how to play this thing!"

Mr. Tiddley-Stink, Tommy's dad, came around the corner with a cup of steaming hot coffee in his hand.

"Your mother and I saved up for a long time to pay for that present. We hope you like it!"

Tommy certainly did not want to hurt his parents' feelings, so he nodded enthusiastically and said, "It's great, Dad. It's really cool!"

Tommy wondered what he was going to do with a guitar, when he suddenly got a great idea.

"Thanks Mom. Thanks Dad. This is the greatest gift I have ever received!"

He grabbed the guitar out of the box, along with his 'Learn to Play Guitar' book, and ran up to his bedroom. Tommy thought that if he practiced for a little while and learned how to play, he could take his guitar and guitar case out on the street and sing for people as they passed by. He imagined that he would be so good that people would start throwing money in his case. He could save up for his own video game player!

For the next hour Tommy practiced playing his guitar. It wasn't quite as easy as he thought. His fingers began to hurt and were getting tangled in the strings. Although it was tough, by the end of the hour, Tommy was sure that he had mastered the guitar. He ran downstairs to the family room and confronted his father.

"Hey, Dad. Do you want to hear a song? I just learned it. I think you'll really like it." exclaimed Tommy.

"You can play the guitar after practicing for an hour?" said his father. "My son must be a genius," Mr. Tiddley-Stink thought. "Okay, Tommy, let's hear it!"

Tommy's father sat down on his favorite chair as Tommy sat across from him on a wooden stool, placing his guitar on his knee.

"Here goes," said Tommy. ***BLARE!!!! TWANG!!!! BONG! WACK!***

Tommy's father dropped his coffee, which went all down the front of him, clapped his hands over his ears, and rocketed out of his chair. He moved as if his bottom was on fire. The problem was that the boiling coffee had landed on his lap.

"Oh, my goodness, Tommy! I think I need to go upstairs and change my pants. I may need some ointment for my legs. Why don't you go outside and play for some of the neighbors!"

Tommy, who was a little discouraged by his father's reaction, put his guitar in its case and ran outside. He soon realized that he was still in his... . underwear? You have never seen a boy run as fast as Tommy did to get back into the house to get his clothes on.

"See you later, Dad. I am going into town so I can play my guitar for the town's folk. I'll be back in a hour."

"Take your time, son. I will be upstairs recuperating... . I mean relaxing. See you in a while."

Tommy walked up Elm Street and was about to turn on to Oak when he spotted his favorite teacher, Mrs. Finklestein. She was walking her pet dog, Pooky. He was a miniature Chihuahua that looked more like a rat on a string. Tommy stepped behind a tree, took his guitar out of its case, and waited to surprise Mrs. Finklestein with a funky version of "If You're Happy and You Know It." Just as Mrs. Finklestein passed by, Tommy jumped from behind the tree.

"Check this out, Mrs. Finklestein! You're going to love it!"

BLARE! TWANG! BONG! WACK!

Pooky flew into an oak tree and Mrs. Finklestein jumped a mile in the air, screaming an ear-piercing shriek into Tommy's ear. She turned around, and whopped him on the head with her purse.

"What did you do that for?" screeched Tommy, as he rubbed his head. "I thought you liked me!"

Mrs. Finklestein just glared at Tommy. Her dress had wrapped around her neck and her wig had flipped around backwards. Pooky was dangling from a branch of the oak tree, hanging on for dear life. They did not look very happy. Tommy quickly turned around, grabbed his guitar case from behind the tree, and headed down the street.

"I'm going to play for someone else who really appreciates my style!" he said.

As Tommy walked a little further down the street he noticed his principal, Mr. Freud Ian Shlip. Mr. Shlip was standing in front of the ice cream store, buying a Triple Chocolate Ice Cream Blaster. It was huge! He was just about to take a lick of his triple scooped chocolate mountain of ice cream with whipping cream, gummy bears and smarties, when Tommy snuck up behind him and began to play his song!

BLARE! TWANG! BONG! WACK!

Mr. Shlip got such a fright that he ended up shoving the ice cream up his nose. The chocolate ice cream, Smarties and whipped cream were hanging from his nostril. The cone had positioned itself on his nose to make him look like the Wicked Witch of the West. He was not very happy! He turned around and gave Tommy his meanest look. His eyes were bulging and his hands were clenched. Mr. Shlip was furious! Tommy's eyes widened and his mouth dropped to the floor. When Tommy attempted to say how sorry he was, he found himself unable to utter a word. Tommy was starting to think that maybe, just maybe, he needed to practice the guitar for more than an hour. He packed up his guitar and was home in a matter of minutes. Tommy rushed in the front door of his house, stepping on Petey, the hamster.

S-Q-U-I-S-H.

"Petey! I told you not to hang on to my shoe, you silly hamster! I will play with you later", laughed Tommy.

"What's the rush, son?" said Mr. Tiddly-Stink. "It looks as if you have been running from someone."

"I just need to practice my guitar for another hour. If anyone calls, I am not here!" Tommy yelled.

Mr. Tiddly-Stink was a bit of a performer himself. He loved magic, but most of all enjoyed playing practical jokes on people. He would put cellophane on toilet seats, Vaseline on door handles and shaving cream on unsuspecting sleepers. Tommy's father especially enjoyed making things appear and disappear.

"I'm going into town, Tommy. I need to get a bit of magic out of my system. I'll be back in a couple of hours."

Mr. Tiddly-Stink walked past Mrs. Finklestein, who was trying to get her dog out of the oak tree, and Mr. Freud Ian Schlip who was pulling gummy bear remains out of his nose. These were weird sightings, but not uncommon in the fantastical town of Finkle.

Music was echoing in the streets. Someone was singing an Italian aria. As Mr. Tiddly-Stink turned onto Fleet Street he saw Luigi perched on a ladder, painting a huge store sign.

Luigi was singing away, "Oh, sol la mio... Oh, sol a mi".

Mr. Tiddly-Stink wanted to share his magic with Luigi. He walked up to the ladder and touched the ladder with his magic wand. ***Boop, boop!*** The ladder disappeared, leaving Luigi suspended in mid air. Luigi let out a "Mama mia!" and fell headfirst into his bucket of green paint.

"Oh, Mama mia, a spicy meat-a-balla!" yelled Luigi, "watsa goin' ona!"

He sat on the ground with a bucket of paint teetering on his head. There was paint covering his entire body. He looked like some sort of green, alien creature. Luigi looked through the green paint that oozed down his scalp to see who had made his ladder disappear. Luigi could see Tommy's father running down the street, laughing hysterically. Within an hour, Mr. Tiddley-Stink had made the Mayor's hairpiece, a police officer's pants, a little boy's favorite spinning toy all disappear. The people of Finkle were in an uproar.

"Something has to be done!" shouted Luigi. "Tommy and his father are driving everyone nuts!"

That evening the entire town gathered in the town square to decide on the fate of Tommy and Mr. Tiddly-Stink. The towns folk were getting tired of the practical jokes and funky guitar solos. The townspeople decided that the Tiddley-Stink family was to be banished to the other side of the valley. They would not be able to bother anyone there. It was miles away from everything and everybody. They nominated the owner of the local deli, a little, wee man by the name of Pedinky Dinklebaumer, to go and tell Tommy and his dad that they were no longer welcome in town.

Pedinky went up to Tommy's house, with the sheriff in tow, and knocked on the door. Tommy greeted Pedinky and the sheriff with his usual friendly smile, which immediately turned into a look of disappointment and hurt. Tommy realized he was different, but did not expect to be treated so harshly.

They packed up their things and moved the next day to a little cabin in the Emerald Woods, which was on the other side of the valley.

Early one spring morning, two years later, as Tommy was playing his guitar on the porch and his father was out in the barn entertaining Tommy's sister and Mrs. Tiddley-Stink with his latest disappearing trick, something weird happened. It got dark. It was as if the sun had disappeared! Everything in the cabin was shaking and rocking back and forth. Things were falling off the wall onto the floor. Tommy looked across the valley and to his amazement and surprise saw Avey Yo-Yo! Avey Yo-Yo was a giant who had been sleeping for hundreds of years in the Finkle Mountains. He wasn't ever supposed to wake up, but something must have happened, because there he was coming across the farm fields.

As Avey Yo-Yo made his way up the valley, he picked up cows as if they were toothpicks, shaking them and saying, "Mmmmm, milkshake!"

He would shoot them through the air and as they hit their destination, he would scream with excitement, "Ah, milk duds!"

Avey Yo-Yo was heading straight towards the town! If Tommy couldn't think of what to do, the town would be destroyed! Tommy realized that although he was small, he could still outsmart a giant like Avey Yo-Yo. He had a plan.

Tommy grabbed his guitar and ran into the valley where Avey Yo-Yo stood. Tommy's father was close behind. Mr. Tiddley-Stink didn't know what Tommy's plan was, but he sure was going to try to do his part.

"Hey, Avey Yo-Yo... down here! I got something for you!"

Avey Yo-Yo looked down and said, "Mmmm, a little boy. I like eating little boys!"

The giant was just about to grab Tommy and stuff him into his mouth when Tommy stopped him by saying, "Wait, Avey, I've got a song for you. I will play a song on my guitar for you. It has your name in it and everything!"

Now Avey Yo-Yo had never heard a song with his own name in it before, so he said, "Well, I'll listen to the song and then I'll eat you!"

Tommy began to strum his guitar and sang a beautiful, melodious song...

Avey Yo-Yo, Avey Yo-Yo,
Avey Yo-Yo, Avey Yo-Yo,
the strong, the mighty
Avey Yo-Yo

As Tommy sang, so did Avey Yo-Yo. He wasn't a great singer, but boy could he dance. Avey Yo-Yo danced and he danced. He danced so much that he began to feel sleepy. The giant swayed back and forth until he finally dropped to the ground with a loud thud. He was fast asleep. Tommy didn't waste any time. Mr. Tiddley-Stink tossed Tommy his magic wand as he jumped onto Avey Yo-Yo's face. Tommy was directly in front of Avey Yo-Yo's nose.

"Ooh, gross! Look at the size of those boogers! That's disgusting!" exclaimed Tommy.

"Giant, you definitely need a jumbo-sized Kleenex!"

With ***swish*** and a ***tish***, Tommy waved the magic wand above Avey's nose. He gently touched the giant and POOF! The giant was gone. Tommy had saved the town.

From a distance, Tommy could hear shouts of excitement as the town folks cheered for him! They saw what Tommy had done. They couldn't believe that Tommy, all 4 feet 11 inches of him, had conquered a giant who was over 100 feet tall. They couldn't thank Tommy enough. Mr. Tiddley-Stink was so proud of his son. He truly admired his son's courage to stand up to such a terrible giant.

The townspeople gave Tommy the key to Finkle and made him honorary mayor. Tommy realized that he had the power to conquer any giant in his life, whether it was a real giant or a problem that seemed giant. He had the power to overcome it. And, so do you!

POOPY PATINSKI

Chapter 10

Peter Patinski was an ordinary eight-year-old boy who lived on a farm outside the Town of Finkle. Every morning at five o'clock, Peter would wake up, drag his tired, aching body out of bed and make his way out to the barn, which housed all of the farm animals. Peter's job was to scoop up the poop. He had to scoop up all the cow manure and dump it into a bucket. He then had to take his bucket and dump it into a huge bin that contained cow manure, which was used as fertilizer for the crops.

Peter was very tired on the morning of the accident. He could barely keep his eyes open as he crawled out of bed. He yanked his overalls over his pajamas and slowly made his way out into the cool, morning air. The sun was barely over the horizon as Peter walked over to the barn to see what messes the animals had made for him. He was greeted by the most disgusting odor he had ever smelled in his life. As he stood staring into the barn his mouth just dropped to the ground. The cows had relieved themselves of the biggest load of poop he had ever seen in his life. Peter was going to be late for school if he didn't start working right away. He moved as quickly as he could. He started scraping and shoveling the manure into his bucket, rushing over to the big bin for the dump. Peter was moving around so quickly that he wasn't paying attention to what was around him. There, in the middle of the floor, was a large splotch of manure, which had fallen out of his small bucket. Peter's foot landed directly on top of this masterpiece. ***SQUISH!*** Peter skidded across the barn floor and hit the side of the manure bin. The pail of manure that Peter was carrying went flying up into the air and came down right on top of him. He had manure all over his clothes, over his head, in his ears, and even in his mouth. Peter ran into the house and cleaned off as much of the manure as he could. He didn't have time to take a shower as he was going to be late for school.

Peter grabbed his lunch and school bag and darted out the door. As he approached the school, the entry bell rang. He made it just in time. As Peter entered the classroom, he noticed that everyone was staring at him and holding their noses. Dirk, Brutus and Billy, the school bullies were the first ones to say anything.

Brutus yelled out, "What is that horrible smell? Is it you, Peter Patinski, farm boy extraordinaire?"

Of course, this led to a parade of comments and criticisms about the smell.

"I think instead of calling you Peter Patinski we should call you Poopy Patinski!" yelled Billy.

There it was, the beginning of the end! From that time on Peter was known as Poopy Patinski, "the boy who smelled like cow dung." How he hated being teased! He would have done anything, if only his classmates would have called him by his real name, Peter.

Brutus knew that Peter hated his new nickname. He knew Peter would have done anything if people would just call him by his real name. So, Brutus got together with his friends to make a plan, which would humiliate Peter even more, if that was possible!

They decided that they would dare Peter to sleep in the basement of the new school that was being built on the other side of the MacDurmit apple orchard. MacDurmit's Orchard was supposed to be full of horrible boy-eating creatures which would scare even the bravest child. There was also the mystery around why the workmen refused to finish building the school. It had been said that as the workmen were laying the last cement slab for the basement, one of the workmen unearthed something horrible. The kids at school said that an evil creature was awakened from the dead. The workers refused to go back, thus, the school had never been finished.

Brutus, Billy and Dirk expected Poopy Patinski to chicken out, but they didn't realize how badly he wanted to be called Peter again.

"I accept your challenge. I will sleep in the school basement as long as you quit calling me Poopy! Agreed?"

Brutus and his friends agreed to never call Peter, Poopy Patinski ever again. What Peter should have realized is that bullies like Brutus, Billy and Dirk never keep their promises. They get kids to do dares and then, back out on their promises. Peter should have known better.

It was about 11:30 p.m. when Peter heard his mother and father turn off the lights and go to bed. He quietly opened the window of his bedroom and slowly lowered his body onto the dew-covered grass. Peter was wearing his warmest coat and had his hat and gloves on. He hoped they would protect him from the cold wind that was howling through the trees and hitting his frail eight-year-old body.

Poopy walked down the dimly lit alleyways that weaved behind the darkened homes of Finkle. Everyone was asleep in their cozy beds. Poopy had a very uneasy feeling that permeated every inch of his soul.

"Maybe I should head back to my own cozy bed?" murmured Poopy. "No, I can't turn back now. I need to prove that I am brave enough to do this dare so that I will never be called Poopy Patinski again."

It was approaching midnight when Poopy arrived at the path that wound its way through MacDurmit's Orchard. It was pitch black. Not even a flashlight would cut through this blackness. Poopy took a deep breath. All he could hear was the sound of his heart beating... beating faster than it ever beat before. There was an eerie silence surrounding MacDurmit's farm. He felt as if he was being watched.

Poopy had been walking for about ten minutes when he spotted something. There were two eyes staring down at him from a tree that was approximately ten feet ahead. Poopy heard a high-pitched screech as this horrible creature flew directly at him. He jumped around as if he had ants in his pants. Poopy was screaming and tearing at his clothes as he tried to pull this evil thing off the back of his jacket. He figured that if he was going to be eaten by this ferocious beast, he would at least put up a good fight. Poopy ripped off his jacket and threw it to the ground. Poopy was so scared at that moment he thought he was going to pee his pants! He expected to see a huge boy-eating creature attached to his jacket. The creature Poopy was so afraid of was a harmless squirrel? It must have fallen out of the tree and got its claws stuck in his jacket. It looked absolutely terrified! He felt kind of foolish

when he realized that the ferocious creature was nothing more than a harmless squirrel. Poopy unhooked it from his jacket and continued on his way to the school basement.

Ahead of him was a clearing. He could see the images of the abandoned construction site looming in the shadows created by the walls of the unfinished school. There it was! The basement in which he had to spend the night. What was waiting for him down the steps that led to the basement? Would the mystery of why the workmen refused to come back to finish their work be revealed tonight? Poopy slowly walked down the stairs, which led into the unfinished basement. The air was musty and damp and the ground beneath his feet was muddy and wet. This definitely was not the ideal spot for a comfortable snooze!

Poopy cautiously rolled out his sleeping bag and was about to slide his shivering body into it when he heard - "the sound." It was the sound of crunching feet moving slowly around the basement edge. His heart began to beat faster. His hands and body began to shake as he never had before. Who was this intruder? Could it be the thing that scared the workmen away? On the other hand, maybe it was the boys who dared Poopy to come down to the basement in the first place. They probably wanted to give Poopy a good scare. He reached behind his back and into his knapsack so he could grab his flashlight. He turned it on and shone it toward the sound that was getting closer by the minute. He stared up the cement stairway to see the image of something very large. It walked on two legs, but it did not have a human form. Poopy began to shine the light on the legs of this creature as it descended into the basement. He noticed that the legs were reptilian. How could this be? He felt as if he was part of some sort of alien horror flick. He bravely began to raise his light slowly to look at the face of his on-coming foe. Just as he was about to see what the creature looked like his flashlight went out! Poopy quickly reached into his knapsack where his spare flashlight lay. Just as he was about to turn around, he could feel that the creature was standing right over him. He could feel its hot, smelly breath hit the back of his neck and its saliva drip onto his skull. Poopy quickly turned around and flashed the light directly into the face of his attacker. ***A-a-a-a-a-a-a-h!***

At approximately 1:00 a.m. there was a blood-curdling scream that echoed throughout the entire community of Finkle. Dogs began to bark and howl as if they were in excruciating pain. Lights in every house in Finkle were turned on, as the scream had awakened everyone.

The next day at school, Brutus and his friends were quick to notice that Poopy was not at school. At lunchtime, they wolfed down their lunches and scrambled across town toward the basement of the new school. As they walked down the stairs, they noticed that there were strange markings in the dirt directly at the entrance to the basement. It looked as if something or someone had been dragged into the forest, where the strange marks ended. Brutus and his gang looked everywhere for

Poopy, but no one could find him. It was as if he had disappeared from the face of the earth.

Months went by and Poopy was never seen again. Many stories were told to explain the mysterious disappearance of Poopy Patinski. Some said that he moved. Others said he was too embarrassed to show his face around school anymore so he had switched to a new school. Still others said that something strange happened that night, something that affected the rest of Poopy Patinski's life.

The workmen eventually came back to finish the school. The new Milmac Public School was created and the old school was turned into a bank. Students were never told about the basement and Poopy's disappearance. It was thought to be better that way.

Barf Barfoni, brother of Eric of the Green Gorilla fame, knew about the story of Poopy Patinski and the basement, because his grandfather had told him about it. One afternoon, Barf was listening to a story in the school library when he began to feel sleepy. For a moment, he lay his head down on the library carpet. It was always soft and warm. Just as his ear hit the carpet, he heard a strange voice coming from under the floor of the library.

"I am Poopy Patinski," it whispered. "I am Poopy Patinski."

It was Poopy! It was the voice of Poopy Patinski! Barf jumped up and started dancing around the library. The other students and the librarian just stared and thought that Barf had finally lost it.

"I hear Poopy, I hear Poopy!" screamed Barf.

The librarian calmly looked at Barf and said, "Listen Mr. Barfoni, if you hear a Poopy you know where the boys bathroom is. I suggest you use it!"

Barf looked stunned.

"Not that kind of Poopy. I hear Poopy Patinski!" yelled Barf.

Of course, no one believed a word he said. Not yet anyway.

THE SECRET BASEMENT

Chapter 11

Barf had never been the same since the day he heard Poopy Patinski in the overcrowded, overstuffed library at Milmac Public School. The librarian treated him as if he had two heads. She had made Barf march to the boys' bathroom although he told her that he didn't need to go.

"How dare she humiliate me in front of my friends. Now my friends think that I am making up stories. They don't believe the story of the secret basement or that I actually heard Poopy Patinski. No one believes me except my best friend, Chico Chic-olet. I met Chico last summer just after he arrived here in Finkle from the country of Chico-Chico. We do everything together. We are going to prove that there is a secret basement and that Poopy Patinski does exist."

It was the beginning of another nauseating week at Milmac Public School. The sky was almost pitch black as Barf made his way to school through the narrow cobblestone streets of Finkle. Snow smothered Barf's senses as he tried to keep his mind focused on what he had to do. He had to prove that there was a secret basement and that Poopy Patinski was more than a figment of his imagination.

The night before, Barf had met with his friend Chico. Chico was the best friend anyone could ever ask for. If you ever needed someone to talk to, Chico was always there to lend an ear. Barf and Chico decided that they would uncover the secret of the mysterious basement and prove that they were more than two under-rated geeks.

Both boys watched the clock in Mrs. Finklestein's classroom all morning. They knew that when the bell rang for lunch recess they were going to undertake the biggest adventure of their lives. The hands of the clock moved excruciatingly slow that morning. As every minute ticked by, the boys became extremely anxious. Sweat greased their palms, but their minds were full of determination and commitment. They knew they could not turn back now. The bell finally rang, marking the moment of their journey into the unknown.

Barf and Chico gobbled their lunches as if it were their last, then raced out to the playground with their classmates. Everyone on the playground grouped together in their usual cliques as Barf and Chico plotted their route back into the school. They often imagined how they would escape the drudgery of Milmac

Public School. Never did they think they would need a plan to re-enter the school.

It was Barf and Chico's lucky day. All the teachers were in the staff room, celebrating the retirement of the librarian, Mrs. Nutter. She looked as if she must have been pushing one hundred years old. It was amazing she could still swallow pieces of solid food, let alone teach a class. She always forgot where she was and began calling her students by the names of her dead cats. People said she had over two hundred cats at her house. Who knew what was true and what was a tall tale? The one thing that was a fact was that she was a wickedly weird woman, who enjoyed embarrassing boys like Barf. Barf never liked her very much and was glad she was retiring.

Barf and Chico crawled on their bellies past the staff room door as if they were on a commando mission. Once they had passed the staff room, they had to get by old Mrs. Pierson, the school secretary. She was a crabby old lady who had breath that was so bad they could have used it as paint remover. As luck would have it, old Mrs. Pierson was fast asleep. Her head was gingerly balanced against her computer screen. A tiny trickle of drool hung suspended from her lips awaiting its descent onto the floor below.

The sound of her snores rumbled between the whiz of her wheezing, adding to the sounds of the snow and wind, which howled through the poorly insulated doors of the school. There was not much time left before the bell would ring and the students would be let in the school again. Barf and Chico got up and ran as fast as they could and entered the boiler room. That was where they thought the entrance to the secret basement might be.

The heavy door to the boiler room swung shut with an enormous bang behind them. There in front of Barf and Chico stood not one, but two boilers. Why did a small, insignificant country school need two boilers to heat its dinghy halls? Something not quite right about this picture. As Barf moved closer to the boilers, he could feel the intense heat coming off one of them, but not the other. One of the boilers was ice cold. A small door on the front of the boiler was partially opened. It begged someone to open it further. The wind outside howled louder as Barf pushed Chico toward the black wrought-iron door to see what lay behind it. Chico slowly opened the iron door revealing a dark, downward-spiraling metal chute. Barf pulled Chico aside to lean in and look for himself. Barf, being a little beefy around the edges, got his bountiful bottom stuck between the sides of the chute. Barf began screaming for Chico to pull him out. Chico grabbed Barf's legs and began to pull for all he was worth. The boiler room was extremely dusty which started to play havoc with Chico's nose. He was trying his best to hold back a huge sneeze, but the dust was just too much for

Chico's sensitive nasal passages. He let out the biggest, phlegm-filled gusher that he had ever sneezed. Barf instantly was cascading headfirst into the black abyss of the boiler. Sliding close behind was Chico, who was holding on to Barf's pant leg. Barf landed first, with Chico's back end landing on Barf's head. They lay on the cement floor in a crumpled heap of flesh and bones. It did not take them long to realize that they were in the secret basement of Milmac Public School. They had found it! Now their classmates had to believe their stories!

Barf reached into his ratty, worn out jeans to pull out a flashlight. The thin beam of light traced the water stained walls of the secret basement. There were wires hanging down from the ceiling with water pipes travelling along the edges of the basement. Chico was sitting behind Barf contemplating the reasons why he had chosen to begin such a hare-brained adventure, when he suddenly spotted an opening in one of the basement walls. Chico pushed past Barf to see what lay behind the hole. Chico cautiously poked his head through the hole to see a catacomb of tunnels spiraling through Finkle Mountain. Barf and Chico had found not only the secret basement, but also an entrance into Finkle Mountain.

The friends slowly maneuvered their pint-sized bodies through the hole in the basement wall. They decided to explore the various caves in hope that they would run across the remains of Poopy Partinski. After all, they didn't expect Poopy to still be alive after all this time. They wandered through the darkened tunnels for what seemed to be forever. Reaching deeper into the bowels of the earth, each tunnel led them into a room that was filled with creatures that inhabited the darkened world. Each step brought a new experience, a new sense of danger! All of a sudden, Barf stopped! What was that sound? It reminded him of the wheezing that came from his old Aunt Flo's bedroom after she had had a few too many grape sarsaparillas. As Barf and Chico inched closer to the unknown sound, they saw a bright light coming from the same room that housed the bone-chilling wheeze. What could be making such a horrible sound?

They peered carefully around the corner of the cave to look into the dark, sunken space. There seemed to be something lying at the side of the cave, but they couldn't think what it could be. A flash of light suddenly blinded the two boys. Then they were thrown into total darkness. They noticed there was a tremendous heat coming from whatever it was that lay in front of them. As each blast of heat focused its wrath on their young bodies, an intense flash of light followed. All at once, Barf and Chico saw the cave wall move. They realized that it wasn't a cave wall they were staring at but a stone-colored, fire-breathing Kimono dragon. It was sleeping along the cave wall. Kimono dragons were not usually this big, nor did they breathe fire. This dragon was definitely a mutant.

From behind the dragon stepped a cloaked and hooded figure. Neither Barf nor Chico were able to see its face. It stood behind the dragon as if it was its master. It slowly reached up and uncovered its head. It was Poopy Patinski! Poopy looked a little older and had long, scraggly hair that cascaded down toward the middle of his back. His skin was covered with dirt and his eyes sparkled with a green glow. Had Poopy discovered something magical in these caves or had he gone mad?

Poopy raised his hands over his head and brought them together. There was a thunderous sound, which echoed through the dampness of the caves. The Kimono dragon instantly woke up and let out a raging screech. It was deafening! The cave shook with the sound as pieces of the walls fell all around Barf and Chico. Barf grabbed Chico and dragged him through the

numerous caves that lay ahead of them. They could feel the heat of the flames chasing them through the endless tunnels. Chico saw the chute ahead of them. Both boys raced as fast as they could to reach their only hope of safety. The caves shook with the roaring of the dragon and the hideous laughter of Poopy. He had gone mad! What other explanation could there be as to why Poopy commanded his dragon to chase Barf and Chico out of the caves?

Barf and Chico flew up the chute, which led them into the school boiler room. Just before Barf's oversized bottom made it through the boiler door, a blast of fire attacked his backside. Direct hit! His bigger-than-large jeans were smoking! As Mrs. Pierson sat at her desk, she could hear two children making a lot of noise, running down the hall toward her. She went out into the hall to intercept the hall runners only to see Barf Barfoni and Chico Chico-let running toward her. She noticed that there were flames and smoke trailing off the seat of Barf's pants. Chico was running so fast that he didn't even notice the secretary standing in his way. Both boys ran right over her. She lay on the school floor with footprints on her forehead, mumbling something about hot crossed buns. Barf ran into the schoolyard, jumping into a snow bank. There was steam trailing off Barf's backside, which came from the fire-breathing Kimono Dragon.

Barf and Chico were always doing strange things, so of course no one paid very much attention to their antics. They tried to convince their friends that they had discovered the secret

basement and had seen Poopy Patinski and an enormous Kimono dragon. No one believed them.

The school day was approaching an end as Barf and Chico stared out the window attempting to figure out a way to convince their friends that what they were saying was true. They noticed a huge van pull up to the school, directly beside the boiler room. Men in white jackets ran into the boiler room and began hammering at something. The boys saw the men drag out about one hundred crates and place them in their truck. After a lot of noise and activity, the van took off. The entire process could not have taken more than five minutes.

Barf and Chico were extremely curious to know what these men had been doing. When the school bell rang and everyone was heading home, they headed directly to the boiler room. Slowly, they opened the boiler room door and stood in the open doorway, staring in disbelief. The second boiler was gone! There was one boiler blasting heat and in place of the second boiler was a huge bin that was bolted to the floor. The secret entrance and the boy's proof were sealed. Why would someone seal the entrance to the basement? Who knew?

Milmac's secretary, Mrs. Pierson realized that Barf and Chico had discovered the secret basement. She had called the Removal Men to take apart the one boiler and seal up the entrance. She could not allow anyone to discover the secret she had been hiding. You see, Mrs. Pierson was Poopy Patinski's wicked aunt. When she was young she was beautiful, but over the years her wicked thoughts and wicked ways washed over her face, transforming her into a wicked hag. When she discovered that Poopy was trapped in the old Finkle tunnels she made sure that he would never escape.

Mrs. Pierson knew that Poopy had been dragged from the school basement by the dragon on the evening of the school dare. She had watched the entire event take pace from her bedroom window. What she didn't know was that Poopy eventually befriended the dragon. It was magical and taught Poopy about the importance of friendship, not bullying others and self-control. Poopy also learned of the magical green dust, which lined the cave walls. This green, magical dust could be used for good or evil depending on who used it. Poopy was going to come back into Milmac Public School and teach other kids what he had learned. He wanted to stop bullies like Dirk, Billy and Brutus from hurting kids with their harsh words and their dares. Since Mrs. Pierson was a bully herself, she wanted to empower the bullies of Milmac, not disempower them.

Barf stared at where the entrance to the secret basement once was and yelled, "I will find a way to help Poopy Patinski escape. Milmac Public School will become a Bully-Free Zone if it's the last thing I do!"

Barf and Chico knew that there must be another way into the secret basement. It was up to them to find the entrance and help Poopy escape. This, however, would be an adventure for another day.

THIS IS ONLY THE BEGINNING

Chapter 12

"Wow! Those stories were great. Can you tell me another Eric?" asked the Green Gorilla.

"It's time for bed. Let's put out the fire and get into our sleeping bags. It's getting late and you still smell like burnt fur. You always find a way of creating another foul smell. You sure are a stinky Gorilla", said Eric.

"I guess you're right. I am getting a little sleepy. I am glad you're not a bully anymore. You're more fun and a better friend now than you ever were."

"Thanks Green Gorilla. You're not so bad yourself. Maybe tomorrow I will tell you about the time I catapulted Bobby Bubblebutt into orbit by pulling as hard as I could on his underwear strap. He became the first human slingshot. Once I pulled so hard on his underwear that I catapulted him head first into a toilet bowl. He popped his head out of that bowl faster than anyone has ever moved. He had toilet paper in his nose, in his ears and on the top of his head. It was a mean thing to do, but at the time, it sure was funny. There are many more stories about Finkle, but that will be for another day. Good night Green Gorilla."

"Good night Eric."

Eric and the Green Gorilla drifted off to sleep. The Green Gorilla began dreaming about Poopy Patinski showing up at Milmac Public School to impart an important message about an evil plot against the students. He also had a dream about the wicked Professor Booten. You see, Professor Booten was an evil sorcerer known for stealing belly buttons. He had always wanted a Gorilla's belly button and was after the Green Gorilla's. Was the Green Gorilla dreaming or were these stories a premonition of what was to happen? The answers will arrive magically in the next book about the Fantastical Town of Finkle.

ABOUT THE AUTHOR

Born in Dundee, Scotland, Graham is an accomplished storyteller, musician and author who captivates his audiences with his energetic style. He makes the likes of Jim Carrey look as if he is standing still, with his hilarious body contortions and his rubber-like face. Audiences are totally absorbed in the tales that Graham weaves about the Fantastical Town of Finkle.

The "Fantastical Town of Finkle" is a collection of stories Graham has been telling since 1993. When he was young, Graham was a poor reader. It wasn't until he connected with someone who believed in his ability to succeed that his interest in reading developed. Graham realized that reading was his ticket to adventure, new worlds and hilarious personalities. Reading also helped Graham develop an imagination that led to creation of the Fantastical Town of Finkle.

Graham wishes to encourage all children to read a book about something they enjoy, so they too can create magical new worlds inhabited by memorable personalities.

ABOUT THE ILLUSTRATOR

Chris Francis was born in Brisbane, Australia and came over to Canada with his family when he was almost 3 years old. After a few years of scribbling on walls and doors, Chris developed his talent at drawing and cartooning. After graduating from high school, he ventured into Classical Animation at Sheridan College in Oakville, Ontario. There he had an opportunity to work for Disney, but declined the offer in pursuit of travel and teaching. Chris continues to have a passion for drawing and painting, marketing his artwork through greeting cards, auctions, murals, websites, and illustrated children's books.